CAPTIVATING THE ESCAPE ARTIST is a modern day tale that explores same sex relationships. A gypsy boy from Algiers meets an aspiring composer-musician in San Francisco. In unseemly settings, the two share lively conversations of odd brainstorming: the etiquette of ants, rude or abrasive idioms, and a condensed evolution of the nature of mankind. Two personal histories span childhood discoveries, the insecurities and masquerades of teenagers, and the highs and lows of substance abuse. Told with self-effacing heart and humor, the two characters mature, showing a capacity for loving and sharing each other in a world worth living in – yes, a world scarred with war, but also filled with magic and wonder.

CAPTIVATING

THE

ESCAPE ARTIST

by Walter Black

Library of Congress: registered
under a collection titled:
*Two Stories are Better than One:
(including) 1. Janey's Story
2. Captivating the Escape Artist*

fiction; same-sex relationships,
cross-cultural partners,
childhood discoveries, teenage
insecurities, substance abuse,
recovery, meditation, visualization

cover photo by the author
back cover artwork by author

ISBN 978-0-615-24984-1

Library of Congress Control Number:

2008908499

CAPTIVATING THE ESCAPE ARTIST

"...the Sage's ability to accomplish the great comes from his not playing the role of the great, therefore he is able to accomplish the great." Lao-Tsu Ts-Tao Ching

I take the Stockton tram to the Veterans' Thrift Store and purchase a crushed velvet cape with a hood. Not that I have a thing for vampires, but it's an admirable cape, and it's raining. I want it. An invisible entity is nudging me; "Get it, get it!" I wear it right out the door. I sense that I need a new environment today, so I bus downtown. Stepping down from the bus at Kearney and California, I gather that downtown is not exactly my fantasy change of environment.

It's drizzling still, so I duck into the Fleur-de-lis Royal Suites. The lobby is recklessly colorful, decked out with gaudy flower arrangements in ostentatious vases of vast bulk. The richness of the interior is a jolting contrast to the drab gray exterior. Through an entryway to the left is a bar-and-grill; *To Be or Not To Be*. The marble-topped tables have ceramic bowls of yellow rose blossoms. The walls and the bar are polished mahogany, carved into vines and grapes. The mahogany is bordered in brass. My velvet cape goes well with the décor.

The bartender looks out of place in severely squared, black rimmed eyeglasses and blond hair pulled tightly back into a frightfully teased pony tail. Her black turtleneck is very beatnik, with a silver necklace that holds an ivory jewel depicting a fork stabbing a lacy snowflake. (Don't ask. Believe me, I didn't.) Some things ornate strike me as malignant.

I pretend I'm in the French Quarters. From the first approachable bar stool, I request hot tea with sourdough bread, and some butter, please. The beatnik bartender smirks, "Walk on the wild side, honey." As she turns with great poise, I see that her ratty ponytail practically extends halfway down the back of her long legs. My barstool seems so alone. I move to a half circle, padded booth under a stained-glass hanging lamp, simulated kerosene. On the ledge beside me is a potted fern that arches over my head. I feel that I'm in my own private cave now. I must appear like a Renoir painting in my oh-so classy cloak.

Alone is really O.K. for me. Unnoticed is very comfortable. I do, however, close my eyes and conjure; *somebody fascinating wants to meet me.*

"Would you like more hot water for your tea?"

I open my eyes and a shockingly beautiful young man in a red beret beams down at me with lustrous white teeth and dark scintillating eyes. He must be the cocktail server.

"Uh, sure."

"Right back."

He bounces over to the bar, almost comically, but with the posture of a good athlete. This guy is the bee's knees. He's the cat's pajamas, if you know what I mean.

"Hot water for the mysterious mademoiselle," he relays to the beatnik bartender.

I'm buttering the sourdough bread into its air-pocket holes. Eee, gad, he thinks I'm a mademoiselle. Why does this most intriguing guy have to be working here, darn it?

He's back with a frilly looking silver kettle. He scoots it across the marble top table with a hand as slender as an artist's. It goes with his elegant face.

"May I join you?"

I pause to rearrange my puzzled expression. "Sorry, I'm not a mademoiselle, I'm a mad monsieur," and I lower the hood of my cape, thinking now that maybe he's not an employee after all.

"My apology, not yours. You are looking so French." His gaze is enticing and his smile is now villainous. His eyebrows are thick and black and his nose is predominant with a pleasing arch. Is he French, Italian, Mayan, or Jewish? He has a goatee and sideburns trimmed thin. There is nothing shaggy or bedraggled about him. His blue-black hair is gleaming and falls long over his forehead, short on his neck.

I think there is some Samurai in him, or snake charmer perhaps. He's sleek and slender and energetic in a jovial manner. When he smiles ear-to-ear he may as well proclaim; "Got you!" He does, and the invisible entity at my side is nudging me again.

RAIN FLAVORED LOLLIPOPS

The dreary drizzle turns to dark silver strands of rope and my glorious cape soaks up water like a sponge blanket, weighing me down. Rajah is shining wet and bristling with daring jabs of humor. He opens a knee-high, rod-iron gate. (We could have easily stepped over the low fence.) A small dingy plot of dead crab grass is embellished with one red tulip that dances a waltz in the downpour. Surely, the tulip is the only visible upbeat touch to his decaying residence: a crumbling slate-pink porch with an ersatz wood-grain door that has diagonal claw marks (hopefully not hatchet marks). There's a see-through hole where a doorknob has been removed.

We bound up treacherous steps skipping two-by-two per leap. In the hallway we leave sinister pools of excess rain water on the scarred wood floors. His room, a tiny studio, lacks its door and the shattered window is covered over with a worn thin army blanket. The greasy carpet smells of dust and puke, but the room is well aired, due to the missing pieces of windowpane. In a flash-pan second, I half wonder if the no-linen, striped mattress we are diving for on the floor might be home for fleas and scabies. Too late for precaution, we are rolling on it. Our arms and legs embrace and our kisses taste like rain flavored lollipops. We stop to gaze at each other, all smiles and mutual amazement.

That night he teaches me a game, called *Rude, Crude, What's Up Dude?* "Pick a word or group of words that takes on extra meaning. What do you call them, idioms?"

"I guess so. Like clichés?"

"Maybe, I'm not sure. I'll give you three examples: plastered out of his mind,…rolling in dough, and,…How's it hangin'?"

"O.K., my turn." (A brief pause,): "head over heels."

"Very good, my turn: singin' the blues"

"He's toast."

"Chill out"

"Pissed off"

"Dirt bag"

"All hot and bothered"

"Pull your head out of your ass"

"No shit, Sherlock"

"That's retarded."

"No it's not!"

"Yes it is, ..no Dumb-Dumb, I mean, that' my turn: THAT'S

  RETARDED."

"Oh, well then: Take's one to know one."

"O.K., let's see: A little bit out there"

"A babe in the woods."

"Jail bait."

"A kid in a candy store."

"Take a number."

"Tell someone who gives a shit."

"I'm so sure."

"Time flies…"

His coat is long black cashmere, open at the neck to the chill that is setting in. Black knit hat and black dress shoes. On the old yellow bike he must have looked like a warlock to the cars that flew by him. Yellow double line. Yellow double line. He's carrying a brown paper bag inside a white plastic bag. Paper or plastic? Paper or plastic? There's a black crystal over his heart that hangs from a red leather necklace. He hasn't slept well for weeks now, he's kicked in the stomach where he's swallowed a football, he's swallowed a fur ball. He's swallowed a fear ball and it won't cough up.

He's pedaling and his coat is flapping behind him. He comes upon a little cobblestone chapel covered on one side with ivy with a circle of stained glass above the door. The door is unlocked and he enters cautiously. No one inside. No one inside. The aisle down the center is carpeted deep blue. On both sides of the alter is the amber glow of a hundred candles. A hundred candles. He's looking for a place to leave the swallowed football, the fur ball, the fear ball. He lowers himself to his knees. He feels the quiet, the calm, the refuge that is this chapel. Like the amber of the candles, he feels a quiet sensation that feels like an inkling of hope.

Maybe he could leave the paper bag in the plastic bag here on the floor. It would end up in the lost and found. He could leave it behind him intentionally; walk out without it and the contents inside. Leave it for the janitor or the pastor or another seeker of refuge. In his mind's eye he sees that this would be disrespectful of the sanction of this lovely place. He has entered here in reverence and so he leaves in reverence, carrying the paper bag in the plastic bag.

The breeze is slight. He feels snug in his long coat with the collar turned up. From the street sign where his yellow bike is locked he sees a row of Eucalyptus across the street. There are large rounded gray stones that look like the tops of elephant heads at the base of the trees. He leans his bicycle against a peeling bark Eucalyptus. He stands in the gulley between the trees and a metal fence. He's looking for the right place. He sets the bag down and lifts one of the rounded rocks. The one he chooses is about the size of a bowling ball. He sets down the

5

rock and takes out an object from the paper bag in the plastic bag. He takes off the newspaper wrapping that protects it. The object is a ceramic mask painted red and black. He places the newspaper back in the paper bag inside the plastic bag. He sets the ceramic mask face-up inside the indenture where the rock had been resting. He picks up the rock and holds it up high, directly above the mask. He says a silent goodbye: "God, I give you my sadness, my loss and my anger. Please take this emptiness that eats me inside." He drops the rock. There is a dulled crash, a crack. For a short moment his arms extend ahead of him like a sleepwalker. He grabs the plastic bag, newspaper, and brown bag and stuffs them into his coat pocket. As he rides slowly home he feels a relief. Perhaps he has finally severed the emotional tie that has tormented him.

A funeral is a ceremony about putting someone to rest. Why not perform a ceremony to put love to rest? He knows he will carry a memory of the little stone chapel and his impromptu ritual of smashing his ex-lover's gift.

(July 1, 1962: Algerians voted in huge
numbers to be free of French rule.)

LITTLE PRINCE OF WALES CLOTHES

Rajah was born in Algeria in the sixties. He lived at first in a tent outside the city, his parents were nomadic hippies and drove a yellow Volkswagen van. His mother was a dark skinned Greek with long brunette hair down to her hips. His father was a milk chocolate Egyptian, most likely the mix of Persian and African. He wore little round gold rimmed glasses on his large beaklike nose. His hair and beard surrounded his face in a huge bulb of black curls. Pot smokers and pill poppers, living like gypsy peasants, Rajah grew up eating a healthy variety of fruits, vegetables, and grains. Shell fish and other seafood appeared occasionally at their camps and Rajah was soon trusted to wander nearby woods and fields and on the Mediterranean coasts he was left free to collect the seaweed and shells and polished rocks. He loved to display his collections of nature on silver trays, sometimes carefully picking a strip of velvet, corduroy, or silk as a contrasting background for his displays. His mother claimed that he had his grandmother's eye for shape, form, and texture. You could grow up to be the curator of a museum, she would say, and in fact his grandmother was a well to do curator in Southern France.

Hippies were a rare sight in Algeria, and Rajah's parents tended to set up camp in the boonies away from city life. Algerians had seen gypsies throughout the century, and the small family passed as such. Algerians are predominantly Muslim, but many speak French as a second or third language, and about one out of ten speak predominantly French. Throughout the century and including Rajah's childhood the country was at war against itself, Arab against Arab. Islamic militants were constantly battling the government security forces. This upheaval somehow bypassed Rajah's childhood as a nature boy. He did learn at an early age that Algeria is part of the Maghrib, which means Land of the Setting Sun or The West.

At age eight, Rajah was left with his grandparents for several years in southern France. His grandmother Emelda had nearly disowned Rajah's mother for her sexually loose ways and her slovenly lifestyle, but Grandmamma Emelda took a quick liking to Rajah and saw to it that the child went to a proper school. Emelda was a wealthy curator of the Musee Barrage de la Verne in the deeply forested Massif des Maures, which is a huge plateau of granite, slate, mica, and gneiss inland from St-Tropez, a glittering seaside town. Near St-Tropez one discovers little coves with golden sand and lively villages.

Grandmamma Emelda's husband had acquired a remarkable fortune in the manufacture of corks for the wine industry. The thick forest of the area supplies abundant amounts of the elastic bark for cork making as well as chestnuts used as a variety of foods and furniture material.

The Musee de la Verne is a short drive from a famous monastery at Chartreuse de la Verne. Outside the museum is a bronze statue, turned mossy green, of a woman soldier with sword in hand, riding a muscular horse. The granite base is inscribed, "A Jeanne D'Arc." Emelda arranged the museum's foyer with ancient daggers and fencing swords along with intricately embossed shields and suits of armor. The spear-headed flagpoles bear colorful flags that split like the forked tongues of dragons. There are ornate candle holders. One gold plated candle holder stands on the floor and looks like a coat rack. In the west wing is her historical display of chairs and tables, canopied loveseats, bureaus and coat racks; all designed in chestnut wood. On the shelves of a dining cabinet with beveled glass doors are antique books with elaborate bindings with embossed designs and gold leaf titles. These books are authored by the likes of Honore de Balzac, Gustave Flaubert, Prince Hermann Von Puckler-Muskau, and Francois Rabelais. The south wing is where Rajah loses himself, marveling at the glorious display of intricately crafted household and sacred items. There is a bejeweled book of sacred text. The cover portrays a barefoot Jesus wearing an indigo robe. He is surrounded by enamel medallions depicting saints. There is a plate and cup used for the communion during the celebration of the Eucharist. The plate is an eleventh century alabaster paten, edged with jewels embedded in a gold rim. In the center, a gold enamel medallion shows Christ holding the Gospels. In Latin, surrounding him, are his words, "Take, eat, this is my body." The cup is a double-handled sardonyx chalice, also inscribed with Latin characters that read, "Drink from it, all of you, for this is my blood of the new covenant." Rajah envisioned in these relics the practice of witchcraft and wizardry. To eat this man's body, and drink his blood! Were these people cannibals or witchdoctors?

The east wing features paintings from the fourteenth through sixteenth centuries of elaborately dressed soldiers and the immaculately kept courtyards of royalty. Some of the paintings were like windows with shutters, and the hinged doors contained extended parts of the central painting. Some paintings were displayed on cumbersome mahogany or chestnut easels that could be rolled away on their wheels had they not been secured to the floor. Grandmamma Emelda explained to Rajah that artists long ago had unveiled their masterpieces by opening the shutters as if opening a window, unlike today's artists who merely lifted a velvet cloth or satin covering.

Emelda expanded on her fortune by purchasing paintings from Italy, Austria, Spain, Belgium and Holland. After showing them at the Musee Barrage de la Verne for a season, she then auctioned them in St-Tropez in an abandoned fishery for exorbitant prices.

To be sure, Rajah spent much of his time in school adjusting to the discipline along with the peer pressure to "be a man" and to "be a Frenchman" at that. School was painfully challenging after growing up so wild and anything goes, but Rajah easily kept his self respect. He had within himself, if not socially, the spirit of a conqueror. It was the world of Grandmamma Emelda's that captured his admiration and the Chateau de Grimaud, Emelda's castle by the sea, which quickly became his home sweet home. The Chateau de Grimaud was secluded as they usually are. This castle was actually somewhat inland from the sea. The highway that passes the tall gates at the far end of the long driveway heads east to St-Tropez, and winds west to the monastery. If not for the highway, the Chateau de Grimaud was completely surrounded by the thickly wooded hills and vales.

Being a small child, and to a degree untamed, it was a natural curiosity, not wealth, that drew Rajah to his grandmother. A love for collecting and arranging things is what made Grandmamma Emelda a magician in Rajah's eyes, and Emelda grew to love him dearly. This friendship was to be a financial boon that would last Rajah a lifetime, and had he ever chosen to live like a king, his namesake, he could have easily afforded it.

Emelda became in her lifetime a local icon for the illustrious auctions at the old fishery, primarily because she had a refined taste for the excellence and authenticity of artwork, and she could afford to buy out her latest discoveries over and over again.

Emelda bought Rajah new outfits. His mother, Germaine, would have laughed at the transformation; gray herring bone double breasted sports jackets with matching golfers' berets and lamb chop shaped jockey shorts with bands below the knees above long argyle socks that disappeared into shined shoes with big square buckles. Germaine would call them rich kid clothes, the Little Prince of Wales clothes. Rajah looked like a character right out of a storybook.

And the Chateau de Grimaud, his new home, was a wonderland. It was a literal castle surrounded by rolling lawns that tapered into periwinkle creeping myrtle and Italian cypress trees that looked like massive green feathers; curving cobblestone pathways that meandered among crescent shaped ponds edged with cattails with gliding black swans that would honk like wild geese. The pathways circled several large ornate fountains with statues of shining black nymphs, dancing frogs and dragonflies suspended in the spray of water. There were mazes of hedges nearly overrun with the vines of crimson nasturtium and silver fleece. Brick walls were laced with star jasmine and morning glory. Along one wall was a manmade brook and at every turn were banks of asparagus fern with its soft fine foliage. The driveway was a gravel of polished rock lined with trellises of roses and old oak trees with branches that arched high over the drive like a tunnel.

ARRIVALS / DEPARTURES - San Francisco 1975
(1974) President Nixon avoids impeachment by quitting.
(1975) Movies: *JAWS* by Steven Spielberg
ONE FLEW OVER THE CUCKOO'S NEST (wins four Oscars)

The Greyhound bus pulled into Oakland before the sun rose. The A.C. Transit bus shuttled San Francisco-bound passengers across the double deck bridge. This bridge inspired a later nightmare about a bridge that curved up and up until I was driving straight up to where the bridge ends up in the sky like a theme park thrill ride. The old rundown bus station on Mission between Second and Third Streets has old wooden pews. It looked like a film about Ireland in the morning light, dark and golden and empty except for a bum asleep on the bench. The bathroom stalls were trashed. Where were the gay men and young guys? I went out on the street where everything and everyone looked exhausted and mid-western (exactly what I had hoped to leave behind).

I bought a Chronicle and crossed Third Street to a small dive of a coffee shop (probably Cup o' Joe). The golden morning poured over the dingy place with its horseshoe Formica-top counter and swivel pill-box chairs. Nothing there looked redone or re-upholstered for a retro flare, just plain rundown and cheap. I ordered French toast and milk and went through the ads for rooms for rent. I rarely looked at the front page news let alone read the paper. I found a cheap hotel called Grand Central and also a Bachelor's Quarters with a sauna, even cheaper, $65 per week. Or was that per month? It was nearly thirty years ago, so it was probably the monthly rate.

I set off with my mother's old suitcases for the one with the sauna. I loved the idea sweating it out and paying less. I had a map from the bus station and figured I could walk. I was twenty-one, in blue jeans and shiny shoes, crossing Market Street into the financial district. The neighborhoods changed from one block to the next from rundown greasy spoon into grandiose skyscrapers, modern banks, well-kept hotels with doormen in Henry XIII costumes. The sidewalks had saplings evenly planted. There was no big hustle-bustle of the rush hour traffic.

11

Either I missed it or I was too self absorbed to notice people. I remember the mammoth slabs of architecture and the incredible weight of my suitcases.

I walked up Stockton Street through Chinatown. Now I was overseas, a tourist or a journalist on assignment. It may have been densely crowded, but I felt transformed and forgot about the weight of my luggage. Little trinket shops beckoned with pagoda entrances, lots of gold and red, and Chinese writing like tarantula poses. There were new smells and a new sense of space (or rather a lack of space). There were turtles in barrels and silver fish in wooden boxes, ducks on hooks without their feathers, and lots of feet shuffling around in black canvas shoes.

The neighborhood changed again and I hadn't walked many blocks. Now I was passing strippers and peep shows, neon signs with blinking nipples on a neon girl in a topless bikini and high heels. I trudged past doorways with flashing lights and black curtains and barkers - young antsy men in not-quite-right suits (too flashy, too mismatched, or didn't-really-fit) and wearing too many gold chains and rings. These barkers wore quick stabs at the look of success, but the suits went with the blaring voices, "Slits, clits, and lots of tits". I should have yelled back at them "and unshaved pits", but I had no personality back then, in fact it always took a few beers for me to make conversation and it certainly took more than that to get me on the dance floor those days.

The Bachelor's Quarters was on Grant Avenue and once again the neighborhood changed. It was North Beach, home of the old beat poet, Italian coffee houses and a nautical bar with Irish jigs called Specs, and Vesuvio's, the Italian jazz bar named after the volcano. Next to Bachelor's Quarters was a slam-bam get-down blues bar. North Beach had old Victorian houses wedged here and there. Bachelor's Quarters had a black door with the address on a silver plate. The manager answered to the buzzer. Harry, a bookish little balding man, upbeat and brisk, greeted me. The rooms were about the size of horse corals with single beds each, one shower per hallway, two toilets; one by the shower and the other at the opposite end of the hall. The room had a porcelain sink that fitted the corner, funky wood plank floors, no built in closet, with a double door metal wardrobe pasted over with dark wallpaper for the intended look of wood.

12

The whole three floors of the place verged upon being the crash pad for strung out beat poets, but the few guys I met were alive and well enough to not seem downtrodden. Harry introduced me to Shri, whose door stood open. Shri had dark hair and a beard, wore a Chinese silk robe with black satin trim and blue jeans. He had a sea green velvet shawl draped over his dresser with a gold Buddha and musk incense. Trinkets, bells, and wind chimes hinted at the presence of magic. There must have been a bag of marijuana somewhere in the room. Shri smiled and his teeth were pearly white. He wasn't skinny, he looked cuddly and exotic. Back then he looked like the good boyfriend type (although I'm sure I had yet to conjure up "my type" as yet).

I investigated the Grand Central Hotel next. It may have been central, but it was far from grand. The place had "housatosis," it smelled like old people and looked even more dreary. The tenants must have all been waiting to die, it smelled like gastric influenza, and looked too uneventful even for strung out beat poets to bother with it. The desk clerk didn't introduce me to any of the tenants and he was probably doing me a favor.

I ended up at the Bachelor's Quarters. Why lug around the suitcases more than I had too? We had our little socials in the first floor's kitchen fixing breakfast or dinner. Nothing was ever safe in the fridge and I learned to buy milk in the evening, and leave it out on my window ledge. Within days I realized the place was exclusively gay in a mixed neighborhood of strip joints for the sailors, Chinese and Italian food galore, and the straight bars I mentioned. The neighborhood was not at all gay, but "anything goes" was the nature of North Beach.

....

One morning I was eating cereal in the kitchen and Harry came in with a mop and bucket, fixed his hot water for the instant Maxwell House freeze dried. He was stirring with his spoon, "O.K., little crystals, do your thing." He asked me if I had a lover. I told him no, I had never had one. He said I would.

During the first few months I lived upstairs on the west side of the building. There was a loud blues bar down below, next door and some mornings at three a.m. a loud, obnoxious drunk would start ranting in the alley below my window. I learned to

13

throw out water from my window out of a large pan. There would be cursing and jumbled threats, but the guy would end up leaving before he'd get soaked again.

One spindly tenant with short cut blond hair like a lioness and sinister tarot card eyes told me that I descended from royalty. (Something about the shape of my head, he claimed.) I didn't mind this sort of speculation. We were talking about far away things, so I told him about the dream I had the night before I boarded the bus for San Francisco.

Throughout childhood, I had a reoccurring dream that I walk down the street, go into my house, and then realize, "Hey, this is not my house!" so I run into the bedroom of the stranger's house, jump on the bed, bury my face in the pillow and start pounding the bed until I wake up. The dream had evolved into repeats of this with me waking up and then realizing that the room I woke up in was also a dream. In desperation to really wake up I would pound the pillow with my fists to jilt myself awake.

The night before my departure, I woke up suspended in mid air above my bed near the ceiling and realized I had no arms or legs, no body at all. I assumed that it was my usual trick dream except that the bedroom in the moonlight was actually my bedroom. Then it occurred to me that I was dead! I wondered if time had come to a stand-still, or I had come to a stand-still and didn't notice weeks and months flying by. My mother could have been in and out of the room dusting and vacuuming a hundred times and I was unable to see her because I had become this eternal eye suspended near the ceiling.

I felt alarmed at either possibility. My instinct to pound the bed with my fists set in. How could I pound the bed with no hands? I decided to pound myself in the face, but again, no hands and no face. By now I would have screamed if I had a mouth for screaming. I visualized with some intensity my fists pounding my face and there was a sensation like sponge hands pounding a sponge face. I could also visualize my dead body below, lying face up on the bed (or hopefully my sleeping body on its back).

I then saw suddenly a large blur to my right. It was my thumb and I was face down on the pillow, not face up as I had imagined. The sight of my hand startled me awake and I pushed myself up into a sitting position. I wanted to make sure I wasn't dreaming; that I was awake. I felt convinced - definitely, I was no longer dreaming. This was my real room and I was awake, but this time it was not the usual relief because the room looked exactly the same as it had when I was suspended without body. The same moonlight, the same eerie but normal room I was used to sleeping in looked as real and yet as disturbing as it had while I was dreaming.

The short haired tenant with tarot card eyes said that my experience was not a dream. It was astral projection and I had really left my body. This sounded believable to me. He asked me if I had traveled through the walls. Well, no. I was too horrified to do anything but try to wake up. "Next time you astral travel," he advised, "try moving about, because you can move through solid objects when you have no body." I told him O.K., but I was thinking that I don't really look forward to experiencing this again.

Dusk and silhouettes of poison berry shrubs along the peeling picket fence. A sidewalk between bungalows leads to the two-car garage. The walk-in door left open looks less suspicious. No, close it, better. There's a convertible sports car and a lumpy looking car covered with a beige canvas.

Hubcaps cling to one wall, massive bags of cat food and laundry soap boxes clutter old shelves. A redwood ladder leads up to sleeping bags and folded jackets for pillows. The two lovers are talking:

It goes back to the cavemen days. A man claimed a cave as home. He'd spot a woman, perhaps she was with her family or her mate. The caveman had to beat up or kill the father or mate, or drag her away from her sisters by the hair to his cave-home. She became a belonging of his, like a log chair or a cave drawing on the wall. He may have been quite brutal in convincing her of this. He may have clubbed her on the toes if she stepped foot outside the cave.

She learned to stay put and make do with the fire and cooking dead animals that he dragged home. If a minimal amount of trust developed, she was allowed to pick berries near his cave or pull up roots from plants adjacent to the cave-home. She started to crank out a few cave kids, who, no doubt kept her occupied while he was out carousing.

He fooled around on her?

Probably. This wasn't any formalized marriage so much as the caveman just being a ruthless pig.

Things haven't really changed, then.

Hey, now there's alimony and child support. Anyway, he's carousing and hunting and she's at home in the cave, run ragged by her cave kids, unless she teaches them to pick berries and pull roots. Each cave family is the mortal enemy of other cave families. But some family came along, probably a big family with a big cave - and I wouldn't be surprised if it was a couple of cave sisters who started arranging the berry bushes and root plants and maybe even discovered that fruit seeds and flower seeds make new plants, and lo and behold, they started agriculture. This increased the food supply and therefore the family size grew, and cave families who were nearby neighbors may have figured out to stop killing and attacking each other, and form a little tribe, which the cavemen noticed was more powerful than a cave family. But they were brutal pigs and the men had battles to decide who would be the tribe's leaders, and lo and behold, we had the birth of politics.

Which is still the battle of brutal pigs.

Pretty much. The tribes divided up the work into women growing food or picking or pulling food and the men going hunting. Most of the women didn't like killing anyway. Eventually, growing plants got big enough for the tribes to form towns, and then each town was the enemy of other towns. The brutal pigs from one town would conquer other towns, which was a slight veering off from just hunting animals. The conquering brutal pigs collected enough towns to form a state.

All this collecting of towns and conquering other states pretty much got limited to the general landscape of oceans and severely steep mountains or deadly deserts. Pretty soon, the conquering and collecting of power and the overall pigging-out of the fiercest leaders formed nations who considered other nations "the enemy".

In the midst of all this town collecting and nationality formation, there were kingdoms ruled by kings who made the laws and everyone did what the law said, which really goes back to the original caveman telling the cavewoman to stay put or he'll pound her toes black-and-blue or pull her around by her hair some more.

Sado-masochism.

Pretty much. But kings got old and feeble and overthrown, or they just croak, and new kings took over. The local cavemen who had upgraded to huts and shacks and slums and ghettos started talking about kings that float around in the sky - who are still perfectly capable of beating your toes and pulling your hair, and you better not cry or he won't fill your stockings with toffee and lollipops, and if you really play your cards right, you get to go to Wonderland in the Sky. But, if you sneak around outside the cave while the cave king in the sky isn't looking, he'll throw you into the mouth of a live volcano and, (get this, speaking of sadism), you won't die in the burning lava, you'll burn on and on and on, ad infinitum. It sounded bad enough that it kept everyone from sneaking around while the real king was taking a shower. And to capitalize on sadism, they came up with a cave king in the sky who never slept, and never took showers. He just sits up there watching your every move. It worked for a few people, but most of them were sneaking around like rebellious cavewomen everywhere you looked.

At one point in time, it looked as if the nations, brutally bashing other nations, divided into one-side-of-the-planet against the other-side-of-the-planet. They called it The Cold War. We've been waiting for aliens to unite us as one planet against an exterior enemy, but it's been a while now without the appearance of an exterior enemy, and meanwhile, things are digressing back to nation against nation as the general who-is-the-enemy plan.

"Blessed are the meek, for they shall inherit the earth."
Delivered by Jesus, *The Sermon on the Mount*

THE CHESTNUT CATHEDRAL

Rajah is free to roam the grounds with a nanny who escorts him if and only if his studies are complete. Inside there are butlers and maids, a chef and kitchen staff. The newly hired nannies check on his studies and keep an eye on his playtime. Rajah has a fountain pen and an inkwell, on a roll-top mahogany desk. His fingers are frequently blue with ink that smears on his paperwork. He is patient for a young boy and soon learns to be especially careful. Outside with his uniformed escort nanny he collects acorns and rosebuds and odd pebbles from the driveway. He's always anxious to show Grandmamma his collections and she asks him about his schooling and does he have any new friends and what's his favorite subject and what does he think about clam chowder with fruit for dinner and on and on with more questions than he's ever been asked in his whole life.

Occasionally as he wanders the grounds he sees a little girl with bright orange hair. She is always passing outside the huge gate entry to the Chateau de Grimaud. She looks perhaps five or six years old, and she pulls a green wagon. She wears a checkered apron tied around her white dress and her skin is radiantly white. Even on a gray day her complexion is so milky that she seems to have a white blur about her, a ghostly quality that Rajah finds alluring. He always stops to take in a long look at her, but then he must also himself be quite a sight as the little girl stands motionless gazing at him. The little girl has never added to his collections and she is certainly not part of his studies or dinner, so she remains unmentioned during Grandma Emelda's inquiries.

One late afternoon Rajah is outside by the fountain with Mimi, the largest of four nannies. The day is overcast but not dreary because of the lushness of the surroundings. Rajah is on his stomach on the ground working on rows of multiplication problems mixed with addition problems that involve carrying a one in the tens place. Mimi is on a bench with her never ending knitting spread out on her lap. Nearly to the last row of problems, Rajah hears a rough snort that sounds like a horse. He looks over his shoulder to discover that Mimi has nodded off, snoring again like she did last week. She must have taken a good twenty minute nap sitting up last week. Rajah finishes the row of problems and then gets up to take a break. Mimi lets out another loud honk that sounds like Grandpa blowing his nose. Her plump double chin serves as a good pillow against her puffed up chest. Rajah leaves her be. He tucks his homework into the math book and places it beside the napping nanny. He follows the cobblestones to the driveway and starts picking through the little polished rocks he loves to sort. Today he saves the white ones in his pockets. As he nears the entry gate he hears a squeaking sound, and looks up to see the little girl with orange hair pulling a squealing rusty green wagon. They both stop dead in their tracks. After about ten seconds Rajah walks to the gate and looks into the girl's wagon. She protectively picks up her baby doll that she has bundled in a quilt. There remains in the wagon a giant pinecone. Rajah says, "Wow, look at that. Where did you get that?" The girl points across the road. Her answer is wordless, just her finger pointing to the trees.

They are both young enough to bypass manners, and they neglect introducing each other. Rajah asks her if she would give him the pinecone. She shakes her head firmly no. He offers her some white rocks from his pockets. She looks dumbstruck at the rocks but still won't part with the pinecone. She points again across the road. Rajah discovers that if he turns sideways he can squeeze between the black bars of the tall fence. He barely fits and the bars pull tightly on his ears but he makes it outside the fence to where the glowing girl is. She points again across the road. Rajah looks back over his shoulder and then left and right before dashing across the two lane road. On the other side there is a shoulder of dry dirt banked with a small clearing of orchard grass with its tiny plumes that are feathery soft to his touch. A few steps more and there are dried wild oats with spikelets that scrape his socks and pants. Closest to the road are birch trees with yellow leaves shaped like coins. The white bark of their trunks are edged with black. A few feet beyond the birch trees are hemlock and laurel grown thickly together and the ground is covered with a net of crisscrossing English ivy. He sees taller evergreens beyond, so he walks further until he comes upon black pines and blue cedars. He finds a few small pinecones, but none that compare to the size of the little girl's gigantic pinecone. The air is misty and cools his face and hands. Beyond the black pines and blue cedars are yet taller longleaf pines. He reaches a shallow creek and jumps from stone to stone until he's across, where he finally locates a large pine cone. This one is smashed on one side, certainly less impressive than the little girl's undamaged pinecone. These trees are much taller and the ground is strewn with long needles. Rajah collects some needles and notices that they have all grown in bundles of three. There are no park markers or nursery labels to tell Rajah that these trees are loblolly pines, but the large pinecones he seeks are from the loblollies.

A large crow lets out its caw, caw, caw and swoops low over Rajah's cap. Rajah thinks how the crow must know the layout of the trees and the winding creek like a map, whereas all is new to him. The mist in the air has thickened to a fog that rolls into the forest. Now Rajah hits the jackpot, three giant pine cones in perfect shape. He kneels down on the needle strewn ground to line them up and compare them to each other. He can't wait to show Grandmamma. He feels adventurous and enthralled and decides to investigate a little further. He carries all three pinecones by pressing two against the center one. The scales interlock like teeth. Soon he tires of holding both hands out in front of himself, so he pulls the pinecones apart, damaging one of them. He decides to leave that one for the forest and keep only two.

He reaches a ledge where the ground drops off. The fog makes visibility low, a few feet in any direction the trees disappear in the mist. If Rajah had arrived on a clear day he would see the other side of the canyon, but for now his world is small and misty. He sits down and admires his pinecones. He realizes he's thirsty and better head back. But first he lies down looking straight up at the cedars that disappear into the creeping marine layer. With his woolen cap and jacket, long socks and fancy shoes he doesn't feel the chill of the mist and he dozes off unexpectedly. He is suddenly startled from his nap by the crackling of pine needles and twigs near his head and opens his eyes in time to see a fawn scamper off into the loblolly pines and the darkness that is settling in. Rajah feels a sense of alarm at the thought of finding his way back in the dark. He stands up, stretches, and remembers his new pinecones. One lies directly in front of his feet and the other a few steps away. As he kneels down to pick up the second pinecone, the pine needles slide from beneath him and he realizes that he's sliding off the ledge. He lets out a wail and crashes butt first onto a small sapling that has grown sideways out of the cliff. Looking down he sees that it's quite a drop and he would have easily broken his legs or an arm if he had missed the sapling. Fortunately, there are several other saplings deeply rooted in the cliff soil and he instinctively knows to try out the sturdiness of each before pulling his entire weight up with them. He also makes sure to grab hold of two at a time so that if one gives he'll still have hold of the other. He makes it back to the ledge safely with only a scratch on his leg and a cut on his wrist. He spots one pinecone and feels certain that the other is over the cliff's edge. He settles for the one without a glance back and makes his way back toward the creek.

He's wandered off course somehow. He finds the stream but he cannot locate the stones that he used for crossing the water earlier. He guesses to head upstream, but he fails to discover the same stones. He remembers a pattern of four stones that made the crossing easy. He finds only one large stone in the middle and the jump will take a running start. He backs away from the creek and wonders how holding the pinecone will affect his balance when he lands on the rock. By taking off his jacket he is able to tie the pinecone to his back by wrapping the jacket sleeves around his waist where he ties the sleeves together. The forest is much darker now, so he feels a new urgency for getting back. He makes a running start for the water and leaps directly onto the large stone, falling forward onto his hands and nearly going head first into the water. He hopes he hasn't crushed the pinecone, but he's begun to fear for his own safety more than the condition of the pinecone. He stands up, takes a deep breath and mentally pictures the remaining leap to the other side. It looks the same distance as the first jump, but now there is no chance of a running start. He takes a flying leap and holds a mental picture of his feet barely reaching the dry edge. The water seems to rise up at the last stretch of the leap and he lifts his left leg hoping to only splash his right foot. His right leg goes into the cold water up to his knee and he feels his foot sink into soft mud before falling forward onto the dry dirt he is reaching for. Both his legs are soaked to the knees and he's lost his right shoe in the mud. He feels willing to leave the shoe behind until he takes a few steps in his wet stocking foot over the dark haphazard floor of the forest – too many sharp edges gouging his wet foot. He drags a tree limb to the water and tries fishing the shoe out with the limb, but he's unable to sense the shoe with the branch, so he rolls up one sleeve and barely feels around in the mud under the water's edge and he's quickly found it. The shoe is filled with mud that falls in globs to the ground with disturbing splats and by the time he has scraped the inside out with a stick, he is splattered down the front with mud spots. He heads back for the Chateau de Grimaud, feeling certain that he will at least come upon the highway. His right foot makes a sucking squishy sound with each step and he feels like he's dragging a leg like the Creature from the Black Lagoon.

He doesn't realize that he's made more of a circle than a direct line to the loblolly pines. He now discovers huge chestnut trees that have held fort on this gentle sloping hill for much, much longer than any human life. The chestnuts stand with an expanse of open space between one tree and the next, and in the moonlight and starlit night Rajah stumbles upon a wide circle of six chestnuts. These six impressive old trees have reached for each other in arching branches far above Rajah's head creating a dome of foliage. Inside the wide circle sit four groups of mica-specked granite boulders. Rajah climbs upon each boulder until he decides upon a resting seat. The boulders look white in the beams of moonlight through the chestnut leaves. The fog has lifted. The stars look like diamonds that bloom on the branches above. In the calmness and the grandeur of the moment, Rajah sees this chestnut dome as a cathedral. The bubbling of the creek makes a soothing church hymn and Rajah makes use of this moment to thank God that he didn't fall off the cliff and to thank the forest for the giant pinecone that remains with him.

He leaves the cathedral of chestnuts with a quiet confidence that he is surely headed back to the highway that passes his grandmother's chateau, and as it turns out, he doesn't have to find the highway by himself, and he doesn't even have to slosh very far from the creek before he sees three lights gently swaying ahead of him between the trunks of black pines and silhouettes of blue cedars. As the lights come nearer he hears the mumbling of men's voices and then a raspy voice shouting, "Rajah, can you hear me boy?" "I'm here. I'm right here." Grandma Emelda had called the local police and a search party was sent out by sunset.

Rajah feels a bit embarrassed that so many people had taken up their time to hunt him down, but the relief of seeing people and making it home to a hot bath and a dinner of fish and chips and ginger ale outweigh the guilty feeling. Grandmamma Emelda knew these foods were Rajah's favorites, and she even had Crepes Suzette left over from yesterday's dinner, and Rajah eats six of them as he retells his adventure to Emelda. He makes a snap decision to leave out mentioning the little girl with orange hair and makes up a substitute incentive for leaving the grounds of the Chateau de Grimaud. He creates a little white lie about a white puppy that was nosing about the gate and whining. When the puppy ran across the highway it barely escaped getting run over and Rajah felt obligated to rescue it, but he never managed to catch up with the little rascal as Rajah ran after it into the forest.

He puts the large pinecone on the dresser by the mirror in the guest room that by now is "Rajah's room." The pinecone is a collection in and of itself, because it holds with it his memories of the little girl with the green wagon, the napping nanny Mimi (who nearly lost her job), and Rajah's little journey into the forbidden forest with its crows, deer, pine trees, ivy, the wandering creek, the Chestnut cathedral with its granite pews, the thick fog, and the sloshing wet mud covered shoe.

THE ANT WATUSI

This evening we're on bicycles. I keep a spare bike for catastrophe days when the seat gets stolen, a tire goes flat, or somebody in a sports utility vehicle backs over my parked bike. Rajah rides the black one and I'm on the yellow one. (I don't feel self conscious on a girl's bike, it seems inane to care.) There is a gently curving asphalt bike path through the vaporous eucalyptus trees along El Camino. The path leads down the beach houses along the bay and then cuts through a parking lot to arrive at the wharf. The wharf is a street on stilts out over the water, lined with restaurants and galleries and souvenir shops. Rajah leads me across the beach. We're walking the bikes now because the sand is deep and it gives to our weight and slows us down. Even walking the bikes feels overly strenuous; we're like ants crossing a meringue pie.

We arrive beneath the wharf, where I lock the bikes to each other so we can continue without them. Out on the water's edge beneath the wharf are massive beams that cross in X's that are reinforced with steel plates where they cross. Rajah leads me out onto the beams. Three times we have to shimmy down one beam and back up the next where they meet in the middle. We arrive at a crawl space shelf below one of the restaurants. On the shelf are soda cans and peanut shells, a large blue plastic bowl, and some blankets folded over to make a bed. We sit together at the edge of the shelf dangling out feet. The water slaps the beams about ten feet below us. His little hiding place is a bit of an obstacle course to reach, but from the shelf we see the curve of the shore line and the black and yellow bikes entwined in each other.

"The bikes are making out."

"Yeah, the bikes are getting it on."

A trail of black ants is passing through the peanut shells behind us. We watch how relentlessly they parade.

"They must have found sugar."

"Either that, or they're on the way to an exhibition at a local ant museum."

(I smile.) "It must be a well known artist, an ant sculpture, perhaps."

"No, in this day and age he's probably displaying ant computer graphics."

"They look so sophisticated; they must appreciate style, ant style."

"No doubt they have their own regimen of ant etiquette."

"I think that they're worker ants, off duty, going out on the town."

"And there's a big party, a dance."

"Ant minuet?"

"No, more like ant watusi."

"Do you think a male ant would get buff to improve his sex appeal?"

"Yeah, that's why you see those ants carrying huge leaves and pieces of food twenty times their own size."

"They join an ant gym."

"Their perception is so different from ours that we couldn't possibly observe what they're really up to by looking through their eyes."

"I bet they have ant séances and ant psychics."

"Yeah, ant E.S.P."

"Ant astral travel and ant ghosts."

"I think they're all headed for a cake walk at an ant fundraiser."

IT'S A WONDERFUL LIFE AND A WONDERFUL
DAY IN THE NEIGHBORHOOD

I'm so inclined to tell about my wonderful life this and my wonderful life that, but the next part of my story in San Francisco doesn't go like that. I truly expected, having been born in Kansas, I suppose, that San Francisco would be my Somewhere-Over-the-Rainbow experience. Even Dorothy had a few dilemmas on the yellow brick road and even Oz, in all its glory, had the Wizard behind the black curtain, pulling levers and adjusting knobs, and turning out to be a big fraud.

Through a placement agency I was hired as a shipping clerk for H. B. Savitch and Co. I worked alone in the basement wrapping and unwrapping time clocks of various size and shape. There was a large metal roll up garage door that opened by pulley and a wide driveway that sloped down from the street into the basement. I had rows of metal shelves with various time clocks, some heavy and cumbersome, others that were worn in a round pouch like an army canteen on a shoulder strap for security guards. I had a standup desk for wrapping boxes in brown paper and address tabs to make on a typewriter and shipping records to keep. Cities I had never heard of: Walnut Creek, Atherton, Los Altos Hills, Los Gatos, Belmont, and Menlo Park. The job was pleasant enough, especially since it paid for the rent at Bachelor's Quarters and I didn't go without beer and food. I had my foothold in the mythical San Francisco, so I didn't take that for granted, but time clocks were certainly not my dream come true.

Music was my dream. I had to borrow from a creditor to purchase an electric piano on time installment. I had developed a complex jazz medley inspired by Bill Evans and I noticed that my keyboard was not precisely in tune. I paid a piano tuner and he showed me how the metal rods had little rings on them that slipped up and down. I spent many hours smoking pot and tuning that darn piano and I was never completely satisfied with the tuning. Time passed and my life made little progress; same job, same electric piano, no boyfriend yet. Days repeated themselves and one week looked about the same as the next.

One night at some tacky-tinselly gay bar on Polk Street, I met a handsome young man who held no promise to become a boyfriend or even a one night stand. He had on a suit that gave him a classy demeanor and he showed me a little white pill with an X engraved on it. He called it a cross-top. He told me there's nothing like staying up all night on these and having a drink as the sun comes up. My instinct wanted to say, "Nonsense, this stuff is dangerous," but the guy had this healthy, happy glow to himself. He didn't seem strange or indecent to me. I had been feeling disillusioned about my life ever becoming grand, and my music dreams were at a real stand still. Besides, coffee was failing to give me that get-up-and-go feeling in the mornings, so I bought a couple of tablets.

I held onto a strong sense of responsibility about my job, and the idea of going without sleep sounded like a good start down the wrong road, so I tried one the next morning at work. I wasn't sure that I felt anything until I went out for lunch and ordered a roast beef sandwich. I took one bite and then just stared at it. The sandwich stared back at me. I was not hungry at all. That afternoon in the basement of the time clock company I started dusting and sweeping and arranging shelves of old filthy machines that hadn't been touched or cleaned for years. I even went through a junk pile of broken down clocks piled in a dark corner.

I loved the cross-tops and I don't recall taking the other tablet, but there was a popular saying those days that speed kills, so I chilled my jets and stayed reasonable with my beer and coffee habits. My spirits sagged. Music just wasn't happening for me. More months passed. I didn't fall in love. I was disappointed with the gay bars. Each bar fit a category; a specific type. There was a black bar for black guys and a Chinese bar for the rice queens. There were cowboy bars and leather bars and no-brain disco bars. There were bars for bears, guys who were big and burly and furry. Through my eyes they all looked fat and dumpy.

Which category was I? What type was I looking for? I despised the question, "Are you a top or a bottom?" I had a top and a bottom and I liked for guys to have all their body parts intact. It took me a while to learn to say that I'm very versatile. I didn't really like bragging, so I tended to have a shut down personality until after a few beers when I'd start babbling. You might call my beer dissertations *philosophy-lite.*

I did like Hamburger Mary's, both the food and the cluttered walls that appealed to my stoner mentality. There was a rock and roll bar across the street called The Stud, with everything including the kitchen sink hanging from the ceiling and mannequin parts on the walls. The clientele was varied compared to the other bars; men, women, straights, funky, dressy, old, young, business suits and leather, white trash, third-world, fourth-world, out-of-this-world.

Still, I didn't build my life around a rock-and-roll dance bar. Time clocks weren't making my spirits soar. The only guy I was attracted to at the Bachelor's Quarters was a straight Brazilian with a great smile and a really messy room. Even Shri didn't want to be touched in the sauna.

I painted a picture of a deflating balloon in a flower pot. It was probably a self portrait. I would climb out the window of my room and sit out on the flat top roof, smoke pot and look at the moon. The earth was a nucleus and the moon was a proton. I was riding on an atomic particle. Maybe I was a miniscule molecule in the toenail of a giant man, perhaps a God or maybe an extremely large guy among other extra large people. No doubt, I didn't even register as a flea to him. So my mind turned; belittling thoughts.

I actually got 86'ed from a bathhouse for sneaking a flask of rum in. I would pour the rum into soda cans from the vending machine. Every weekday afternoon was marked by me pulling the chain on the metal door for the garbage man at my shipping clerk job. Then I'd lower the garage door and return to my dungeon, my cement underground. Mr. Time-Clock-Shipping-Clerk. Whoopdee-doo! I became a time bomb waiting to explode, or implode. I was a convict waiting to escape. I was a rat in a trap. The magic of the wide world was out of my reach. I needed to break out, to make a fast getaway. I needed a significant turn of events. I needed a break.

One night, one of the elegant queeny-type tenants at the B.Q. invited to his room for dinner. He had a deluxe, extra large room at the front of the building. He decided to seduce me and I was willing, but there was no real passion, no real desire. So he gave me a lecture, instead, about watching out for guys that will just use me, ("Mom's" bit of advice about the big city). When I left that night, I thought of him as a snake that portrays himself as a caring person. I felt numb and introverted. Maybe he did care and I failed to believe him.

I decided to create some atmosphere in my little room. I bought some nice candles. I woke up early one night and my curtain was on fire. I ran for a pan of water from the hallway shower, because the pan wouldn't fit into my room's corner sink. I dowsed it in time and made sure not to tell Harry. I promptly bought some more ugly thrift store curtains.

This was not a glamorous gay life with a capital G. This was a ho-hum homosexual life with a small h. I decided I needed to collect unemployment so that I'd have the free time to practice the electric piano. I made a plan, and this was it: get dressed up in drag in the morning, go to work and get fired, file for unemployment, and then start composing my masterpieces for future generations to adore and love. I could see that my life would never be filled with joy, but if my music went down in history I would find some comfort in knowing that my life was not a waste.

A Navajo Indian friend of mine had bought me a blond Afro, very San Francisco. The rest of my attire would be conservative, the secretary look. I watched the women on buses and Bay Area Rapid Transit. Low high heels with two toes peeking out were popular. Skirts to the knee, slightly bell shaped, not too tight. Polyester blouses with stripes. Pearls were in. I wasn't finding the right skirt at thrift stores. Nylons were cheap at Walgreen's. I went to a downtown boutique and picked out a creamy white skirt and tried it on in the dressing room. I had two other skirts in my hands, so I stuffed the skirt under my pants. I left the dressing room and hung up the other two skirts, pretended to look for another one for about thirty seconds more, and then walked out. I learned this from a hitch hiker.

The next day I got up an hour and a half earlier to get dressed and apply makeup. It was a lot of work to be a woman and I was scared out of my wits to walk outside in the morning light and catch the bus. I never drank beer in the mornings so I just stayed scared, all the way on the Stockton bus, walking down Mission Street, into the office of H. G. Savitch. Good morning to the secretaries and Good Morning passing the boss's office and Good Morning through the repair room and stomping down the wooden stairs in my peek-a-boo high heels to my dungeon.

THE VAGABOND IN THE EMPTY LOT

The clouds are long stretches of pink cotton candy and the sky is the color of a blue snow cone. There is no such color blue, maybe after taking a hallucinogenic, but Rajah is not high this evening and there it is, snow cone blue sky. He's lying on his back with his hands behind his head. The backseat of the old, beat up Hudson is his latest hide out. The windows are oval; in fact, the whole car is oval and slate gray. The interior smells like burned rug, spilled oil and dry mud. The back tires are missing, and the old Hudson looks like a polished chunk of cement left out in the empty lot.

Most of the year the grass and weeds are dried up and the bits of broken sidewalk show through here and there in the matted straw of dried grass, but now it's late Spring and by a freak of nature and last years winds, the lot has grown dense with flowers in bloom: Four O'clocks and Forget-Me-Nots and Desert's Paint Brushes, along with white, yellow and salmon colored Iceland poppies. The shining little king is surrounded by a Technicolor world. He gazes out the oval porthole at the gradually setting sun, colors deepening and then fading. The mosquitoes are eating him, but he listens to the far off wailing of a freight train and a helicopter that cuts low across the lot. Two ravens alight on the trunk of the old car. They see Rajah, but he doesn't see them, he's passed out.

MEANWHILE CROSSING COLORADO:

There's a luxury train snaking around the steep curves of the snow covered Rockies and about to pass near Aspen. My face is pressed against the cool window and the woman psychologist beside me is reading her novel, *The White Bone* by Barbara Gowdy.

THE HUDSON IN THE LOT:

In the morning Rajah reaches for his plastic bottle of water on the floor, takes three gulps and heaves open the car door that's ready to fall off. He splashes his face and slicks back his straight black hair. There's a little girl out on the sidewalk pedaling her tricycle. Her hair is pale orange and her skin is so white it seems to cast a little white bubble of light around her. She's wearing a yellow chiffon dress and shiny black shoes. They notice each other and both take a good long look, a dark exotic young man in an old car surrounded by a rampage of colored blossom, and an angelic little ghost of a girl on a tricycle. They expect to see each other again and feel no need to acknowledge each other with any more than their eyes.

CROSSING COLORADO:

I wake up and the psychologist lady has left her book on her seat with the picture of a baby elephant. We're crossing the continental divide and the mountain tops are wide and bleak and the air is thinner and it looks heavenly. A kid with extra thick glasses is looking over the back of his seat at me. His baseball cap says Chuck E. Cheese and his blue eyes are magnified to the size of silver dollars. I smile, a quick dry smile, and head for the john.

When I return the psychologist lady is back, and we talk about the Garden of the Gods and Pike's Peak. I end up telling her about the time I took L.S.D. with a neighbor hippie guy. We drove up to Pike's Peak and came upon a gold mine entrance and followed the cave inside a ways. There was a gold vein running along the top of the tunnel, and I realized that at one time it had been molten lava running like the veins in my arm. It reminded me of a Rachel Welch movie, The Incredible Journey, in which she is injected as a tiny person into the bloodstream of a human being. The tunnel made me feel like a small cell in the bloodstream of a living thing. The psychologist lady interjects that the earth is a living pulsing thing.

That's what I was sensing. And it may not have been a belief in God, but it counted as the belief in a higher source in the way that Native Americans think of Mother Earth as sacred.

The psychologist lady said it sounded like a rewarding experience. She started telling me about the elephant religion in the book she was reading. Now I want a copy of the book. She put her nose back in her novel. I pointed my nose out the window where the world was going by. The train was, by now, moving fast along flat land across fields. The fences looked as if they swooped below us, which created a sensation that we were gliding in a low flying plane.

MEANWHILE BACK IN NORTHERN CALIFORNIA:

He's reclined upon the back seat. He looks Hispanic or Arab or Indian (from India). The wrecked car is slate gray, a '39 Hudson; rounded fenders and lovely oval windows. Among chunks of cement (perhaps remnants of a parking lot) there are Four-o'clocks and Iceland poppies and Lobelia, a glorious chaos of color.

He wakes at sunset, his stocking feet poke out the rolled-down window. Torn, neon-pink, cotton candy cirrus clouds hang diagonally against a snow cone blue sky. There is no such blue. There it is, and he's not on a hallucinogenic. It's the real sky…fading now. Night comes up from the earth, cool; smelling like potting soil and rain clouds. A train wails, short; then long. And then silence – forlorn, but comforting. Soon the soft rhythm of crickets cricking, or it could be the stars blinking? Orion's belt crosses at an angle in the oblong glass behind him. The back seat smells like wood polish and shoe polish and mint toothpaste on spilt oil.

He's waiting for something, someone. He has no smokes – he quit that habit, and no beer – he quit that one too. A plastic water bottle waits on the floor. The Hudson's floor rugs are worn to the metal. There's a blissful aloneness. He's waiting for sleep again. There is no hurry, only the whirring of a helicopter far off… gently whirring, then it's gone.

BLOND AFRO AND PEEK-A-BOO
HEELS IN THE DUNGEON

My fate seemed so altered by my outlandish getup. I started sweeping the floor of the basement and humming haunted melodies that sprang from nowhere. There was an older, Latin repairman named Bennie who seemed amused by my antics. He wore spectacles and his hair had gone gray, his belly was big like Santa Claus. He had always flirted with me in innocent ways, like grabbing my calf gently when he had to grab something from a lower shelf. He was the only one to take my outfit in stride, and didn't seem the least alarmed. Everyone else seemed to be avoiding me, and I avoided them.

In the afternoon the garbage man banged on the metal door as usual, so I pulled the door up. In nearly a year we had never exchanged a greeting or introduced each other. Not one word between us. But today he said, "Oh, they hired somebody new!" and "Nice to meet you." I'd never seen him smile before that day. I knew my voice would sound wrong, so I tried for a higher pitched, "Nice to meet you." "See you tomorrow," he said, and jumped on the back bumper of the truck. He banged on the garbage lift as a signal for the driver to take off. The truck had barely started rolling when the guy looked back with a terrified look, like he suddenly recognized me.

At the end of the workday, I was told that Arnold, the company president, wanted to see me in his office. I had no idea what my makeup looked like by then, but tidy or messy, the moment of truth had arrived. I clomped back up the wooden stairs and stood in Arnold's doorway like a cat on a threshold. He asked me to come on in and sit down. I kept my eyes attentive and locked into my poker face, hoping to shield any expression of fear of embarrassment. He said that first of all he had to admit that I was an attractive woman, but the wild hair had to go. He told me that he had spent his lunch talking to his lawyer and had been advised to not fire me or he may end up with Gay Liberation picketing his door. He then reminded me that I had presented myself as a young man on the day that he hired me. He expected me to come to work as a man from now on, starting tomorrow.

He used his experience with management and controlling others to get me to agree to this. Believe me, it took no real effort. I was uncomfortable and hot and couldn't wait to be out of my goofy getup. Arnold ended the little chat with some tagged-on comments about me certainly making an attractive woman, and he sometimes wondered if he didn't have latent homosexual tendencies himself.

I didn't reply to this, I just sat there, deadpan. He said, "O.K., we'll see you here at work tomorrow dressed as a man."

I clumped downstairs one last time in my peek-a-boo high heels, this time to grab a little potted plant that I had decided to take home. As I walked down Mission Street with my purse on my arm and the plant in my hands, I realized that I didn't have change for the bus. I stepped into an automobile tire dealership to get change for a dollar.

My hands were not free. So I had to push the door open with my back to walk in. Thank God, the place was empty except for the two guys at the counter going through a catalog. When I approached the counter, they didn't look up, so I just blurted out, "Could I please get some quarters for the bus?" (I tried not to have a deep voice.) One guy said, "Sure," and he opened the register, counted out quarters for a dollar, handed them to me, all the while not looking up once from the counter.

It seemed liked a relief that they were so engrossed in their catalog that they didn't bother to look at me. I pick up the plant off the counter, walked to the door, turned to push the door with my back again, and caught both guys gawking at my legs. I may have looked lewd or I may have looked sexy, but I had just experienced the indignation that some woman may have felt during a day when men pant and whistle and act ready to pounce, but at the same time lack the decency to show a face-to-face recognition of human respect.

THE PERCUSSIONIST AND THE MANDOLIN PLAYER

Rajah's mother, Germaine, had switched her live-in lovers so frequently that Rajah's father was lost track of entirely. Germaine ran off with a Portuguese percussionist, leaving Rajah in Emelda's care until age twelve. If not for a fatal automobile accident in Spain that killed the percussionist and a mandolin player, Germaine might not have arrived at Emelda's castle in Grimaud to collect her son and then hitchhike across Italy.

During the trip across Italy, Germaine had sworn off drugs of any sort, but her taste for wine and liquid spirits increased considerably. In a small Italian town famous for its leather, she met an Egyptian businessman who convinced her to practice complete abstinence from alcohol. Germaine agreed to marry the businessman within two months of meeting him, and Rajah found himself on a flight to Cairo with his mother, and so began his teenage years in Egypt. By age thirteen, Rajah's eyes were considerably large and brown and filled with mysterious dreams. Although he was quite thin, his other facial features were prominent and balanced his large eyes. Already people were guessing, could he be from Thailand or India?

THE FIFTIES: THE COLD WAR AND CHARGE PLATES

I was born in Kansas, my mother's name was Dorothy (still is), she didn't have a little dog named Toto, but years later I definitely did get blown over the rainbow. It was the early fifties and the second war of the world had ended, but now that the Soviet Union also had the atomic bomb, a cold war divided the world into them-way-over-there and us-right-here.   Senator McCarthy was ruining the careers of publicly visible big names by claiming that they were Communist spies. Department store charge plates that had been stamped in metal were gradually replaced after the first New York issued charge card called the Diners Club. The new card, good for credit in some 22 New York restaurants, had its office in the Empire State Building. The golden age of television saw Elvis Presley's first appearance on television, and Americans were piling up debts on their new credit cards with the faith that a raise, a promotion, a new job and more wealth was on the way.

Inventions galore for the household, the yard, the face, the hair, the body, and the car were advertised on television and radio like never before. Fast foods for the road fueled us for our trips to stores, where we shopped in modern luxury. New homes sprang up faster than ever. We were a society on-the-go with most of the day consumed with distractions, which helped us to blot out the threat of an impending nuclear attack.

I was a little baby, I didn't know or grasp any of this, and yet, all of this molded who I was to become (for better and for worse). Mom would carry me off to a neighbor's house, and everything in the house would be shaped different and the color themes were so different from our own home. All this style and color co-ordination went with the people's clothing.   The character and inflection of their voices went with the style of their furniture. It was as if clothes grew on people's bodies like hair and their furnishings and landscaping grew right out of their fingers like fingernails. Brick houses from brick brains and wooden houses from wooden heads. I remember a turquoise and white striped awning over a quaint cottage house window. It was fresh and cool and like touring an overseas country just to see how unlike our own home was to other folks' residences.

I remember a little grocery store, only a few aisles separated with stacked shelves. There was a toy on the top shelf I wanted. Was it a teddy bear or a doll? My mother looked up at it, but she didn't purchase it. I didn't wail or cry or throw a tantrum. I was easy going, a happy baby. Well, easy going until my little brother came along only eleven months after me. Every year we were the same age for one month.

In a photo album, Mom kept a newspaper clipping. The paper, I believe, was the Parsons Sun. There's a photo of Mom and George, my little brat brother and me, the cute angelic one. Mom's hair was shoulder length in long waves that curl under at the ends. The article talked about how healthy it is for a mother to add a salad to lunch or dinner. Mom had slicked down our hair with a little fan of hair combed up in front.

There are plenty of photos. Dad was a real estate salesman and a jazz musician. He was also a good photographer. One of the best of me as a baby, I'm on my back in a diaper, head turned to the camera with a smile. In the crib behind me is a panda teddy bear standing up. Another of me is at age two; I'm in my underpants sitting in the backseat of our Cadillac on the fold down armrest. Cars still had that rounded forties look then. There's a goofy picture of my dad with five cigarettes in his mouth. He's wearing a white dinner jacket. There's another grainy misty looking shot of him at the upright piano, his head turned toward the camera with a pensive but easy going expression. That describes my dad pretty well; pensive and easy going. It's that innocence-just-before-the-beatnik-era look.

There's a photo of my kid brother George with a black eye. Mom tells me that he had climbed up on the car and that I had climbed up and pushed him off. Apparently I got a lot of practice when he would sit on the footrest and I would push him off. I can't remember any of this. But I do remember two times in my childhood that I accidentally broke something. The first time my parents had flown back to Kansas for the funeral of my grandfather. George and I stayed next door with the neighbor of duplex. I remember the long rectangular house made of blond bricks. It was mid December and I was on the floor, checking out the wrapped presents under the Christmas tree. A little gold globe ornament fell off the tree and broke. It looked like an eggshell, silver on the inside and gold on the outside. The lady who was taking care of us scolded me and I doubted that my Mom would have been so angry. It was an accident.

Another breakage occurred before kindergarten. I was back in Kansas with Mom at my great-grandparents house. It was more like a ranch or a farm than the suburban homes I was familiar with. I was sitting on the couch while the adults were in the kitchen talking. I knew how to turn on our television at home, so I got up and crossed the old fashioned room to the television. The channel knob seemed stuck and broke off in my hand. I felt horrified, and Mom probably insisted that I apologize.

That trip may have been when my aunt Shelley got married and I was the ring bearer. I remember one evening in Parsons, Kansas stepping out of the car to follow my cousins into a corn field. I felt a vibration under my foot, but I didn't look down to see what it was. I was told by my cousins that it was a horny toad. I was not the play-with-lizards-and-frogs type. I never was the daring destructo-type of kid who liked insects and beebee guns. I didn't care for toy army men and war games. My brother George loved running around in a field with his machine gun and blowing up ant hills with firecrackers. I remember a hot sticky day in Wichita visiting our cousins and there were giant turtles out loose in the neighborhood. The boys would find the heaviest possible boulders that they were able to lift up and then drop the massive rocks on the tortoises back to break the shells. I kept my distance. I didn't want to see the damaged turtles and certainly didn't want to be asked to join in. I would have said no to their pleas and they would have labeled me a sissy.

One night I sat with Grandma on her porch swing. I didn't remember ever seeing a porch swing in Colorado. Grandma asked me if I knew what the ongoing pulsating sound was that surrounded us. I told her with confidence that it was the stars twinkling and she laughed. No honey, those are the crickets.

Kansas had something else I hadn't seen in Colorado: lightning bugs, little flying bugs that glowed in the dark. Some people call them fireflies. They truly amazed me, how they looked like mosquitoes with light bulbs screwed into their behinds. I may have been little then, but those lightning bugs looked like something manmade crossed with nature and they still baffle me to this day.

Before I started kindergarten, the doctor had advised my mother to move to a higher altitude for her asthma. That's why we moved to Colorado and thank God we did. Kansas is so flat that you reach its highest point when you drive over an overpass. There's lots of golden yellow wheat, field after field, and reoccurring areas where one sees those black oil pumps that look like giant grasshoppers, seesawing up and down. Thunderstorms are louder there than I've experienced elsewhere. In Kansas, the lightning flashes are brighter and the boom is so loud I'd want to hide under the bed for protection. I never did see a tornado, but I guess that was lucky for me.

I was about four when we moved to Colorado. Colorado has a clean beauty all its own. I'm glad that I lived most of my childhood In Colorado. We hadn't been there long when Walt Disney came out with *Sleeping Beauty*. At my age this movie was incredibly impressive, but once again, I wasn't the rowdy rough kid like most boys my age. When Maleficent turned into a fire breathing dragon and the prince had to cut through the black thorn trees to get past that horrifying dragon, I hid under the theater seat. It was too much for me and I knew it. I had a similar reaction to the *The Prince and the Pauper*. When the two traded places, I knew I couldn't watch the rest of the movie for fear that the pauper would be found out.

One other movie truly scared me as a boy, and that was *The Day the Earth Stood Still*. A flying saucer lands in Washington D.C. and all at once the power goes out in the entire city. People are trapped in elevators and other tense situations, but let me tell you, when the flying saucer opened up, a ramp folded down, and a huge metal robot started lunging down the ramp; I started sweating. Compared to special effects now, *The Day the Earth Stood Still* now looks laughable and fake, nonetheless, I felt edgy, nervous, and truly scared the first time I saw it as a kid. For years to follow, it was nearly impossible to find a movie as scary for me.

Kansas got left behind, but people still detect a twang in my pronunciation of words. Especially telling is my pronunciation of the word wash. For some reason, I say worsh the clothes, worsh the car. One day it occurred to me that this OR sound might be slipped into the word wash for a reason. I also pronounce the state Worshington with this odd OR conversion. I now have an educated guess why. If you say George Worshington you can hear that there is a bit of a rhyming lilt to the sounds of George and worsh.

At any rate, say goodbye to Kansas and hello to the real world's Land of Oz, the land of dreams, California, and the city of black sheep, San Francisco.

Germaine marries Khunfis on a Thursday night in Cairo, the traditional night for weddings and the end of the Muslim week. Both Rajah and Germaine were astonished by the colorfulness and volume of noise. Honking cars, tambourines, drums and women's tremulous wailing blasted their ears. There were musicians and dancers and a shower of rose petals that covered the streets and vehicles and all the celebrants like confetti.

Rajah inherited two brothers and four sisters and amazingly enough, an additional mother. Germaine and Rajah had their own apartment, but easily within walking distance lived Khunfis' first wife Umaima and her mother Gahsha. Gahsha was wrinkled and gray and treated Germaine with a quiet hissing contempt. Surprisingly, Umaima accepted Germaine lovingly and like a sister. Germaine was soon to learn that Umaima was actually relieved to lose all intimacy with Khunfis, and endlessly bitter arguments between Umaima and Khunfis would arise, usually concerning the welfare of the children.

Germaine tried her best to veil how overwhelmed she was with the dynamics of a large family. She did, however, have her reclusive time at her own apartment with Rajah and Khunfis. Her new husband was consistent about staying with Germaine, but he was frequently gone traveling for the benefit and progress of his commerce in leather boots and jackets.

Rajah was quick to learn frequently repeated phrases: *Shoo esmak?* (What's your name?), *Bel hanaa wash sherfaa.* (Enjoy your meal.), *Enshaallah.* (God willing), and *Tasharafna.* (You're welcome.).

He was also quick to learn the that word *aish*, which means bread. It also means life. His favorite dessert was *Umm Ali*, an Egyptian dessert of flaky pastry layered with raisins and nuts with sweet milk. He also liked *Koshari*, a pasta dish of rice, lentils and tomato sauce, topped with fried onions. He had a difficult time with stuffed vine leaves and intensely hated *Bamiyya*, a stew made of okra and tomatoes sometimes with lamb meat added.

Umaima escorted Germaine and Rajah to the local outdoor markets and eventually Rajah felt gradually confident handling Egyptian currency and avoiding the market saleswomen and men who were likely to take advantage. Umaima gave his mother plenty of warning about swindlers and products to stay away from. Rajah and Germaine drank a lot of apricot juice and chai mint tea and Rajah eventually developed a taste for sugarcane juice from the sugarcane pulp. The sugarcane juice was light-green with foam on top and the Egyptians called it *asab*. He learned the currency of *piastres* and *pounds* and collected many of the twenty-five *piastres* coins with their holes in the middle to make a necklace for Grandma Emelda. Of the Egyptian pound banknotes, he loved the one-hundred pounds note the best, with its illustration of the Sphinx.

Rajah had two new brothers, Hassan and Qassem. Hassan was older and very studious. He could always be found bent over his law books with his little spectacles. Hassan looked the most like his father Khunfis, small and hairy and intense. He was already nineteen and still paid more attention to his schooling than watching girls or looking for diversions. Qassem, on the other hand, had a disposition more like his mother's, more extroverted and fun loving. Qassem was fifteen, only a year older than Rajah. Qassem would invite Rajah to take his studies to the coffeehouses, a short stroll down the alley. He would jab Rajah with his elbow and point out girls that he spied hanging laundry on the roofs or opening shutters for a glimpse of the streetlife. Qassem loved to imitate the old characters that frequented the coffeehouse; he could walk like a feeble old man with a cane, or stick up his nose in the air and talk satirical philosophies. He taught Rajah how to smoke from the *sheeshas*, or waterpipes, so that Rajah's first encounter with smoking was with tobacco soaked in molasses and apple juice. The smoke didn't agree with him, and Qassem got a good laugh at Rajah's coughing and his face that turned a sickly shade of green.

Rajah grew accustomed to the atmosphere of the coffeehouse and frequented the same table by himself to finish his homework or read a book. He had a gift for being able to focus his attention where he chose, and the coffeehouse chatter and commotion would rarely distract him. At home with Germaine or alone when she was gone, he was restless and anxious to leave, and although he was unusually reserved, he felt more at ease with the strangers and familiars of the coffeehouse. The coffeehouse was dark inside. The candles at the tables helped light up the pages of his reading and writing. The dark cavernous cafes with their wavering candles gave him a romantic feeling, as if he were a character in a novel.

One evening as he studied alone at his regular table at the coffeehouse, a gentleman at a nearby table struck up a conversation with him about his books. The man was obviously not Egyptian, speaking French with what sounded like a Spanish accent. He introduced himself as Jacob. They talked about Rajah's studies and the novel Rajah was reading, *A Passage to India*, by E. M. Forster. After about fifteen minutes of conversation, Jacob stood up, put on his overcoat and shook hands. "Perhaps I'll see you here again tomorrow?" he half stated, half asked. "Sure," replied Rajah.

Sure enough the next evening, within five minutes of studying at Rajah's usual table, Jacob arrived at the small table nearby. "Good evening Rajah, would you care for another abwa?" "Hello, Jacob." Rajah checked his empty coffee cup and said, "Sure, why not?" with a show of gleaming teeth. That night the conversation started with where-do-you-live and where-are-you-from inquiries followed by a description of Jacob's neighborhood located near *Heliopolis*, a garden city in northeast Cairo. *Helipolis* is known to Egyptians as *Masr al-Gedida* or New Cairo. *Heliopolis* is the product of Baron Edouard Empain, a wealthy Belgian entrepreneur. The joint effort of European and Egyptian architects, *Heliopolis* was completed in the early nineteen hundreds. This garden city draws the wealthy to its shops and restaurants and Jacob lives in an elegant bungalow-style complex on an estate near *Urubu Palace*, the official residence of the Egyptian president. Jacob describes the Baron's Palace, which resembles a Hindu temple, at the opposite side of *Heliopolis*, and also the Byzantine-style Basilica to the north.

Rajah is certain he has not yet seen New Cairo, and asks Jacob how to spell Heliopolis. Jacob offers to show him around if there is a suitable day when Rajah is free of studies and other obligations. Rajah gets a flash feeling of being pounced upon by a tiger, but the instant passes, and looking Jacob squarely in the face (a handsome, gentle face), he offers, "How about the day after tomorrow?" Jacob reaches inside his sports jacket for a small black book, and after glancing at his schedule, responds,

"That would be splendid, in fact, perfect!" They both smile with exuberance and shake hands.

"I must be leaving. Will I find you here again tomorrow?"

"Uh, no, not tomorrow, but I could meet you here the following morning."

Jacob puts his hands in his pants pockets, "Certainly, let's say nine a.m.?"

"O.K."

"See you then, my friend."

Rajah smiles self consciously as he shakes Jacobs hand again. Jacob only grins, as if noticing Rajah's reserve.

As Rajah is walking back to his mother's apartment that night he feels a light hearted elation. It reminds him of the enthusiasm that he had as a boy that day at Grandma Emelda's chateau when he ran across the freeway in search of a giant pinecone. He also remembers stepping from the side of the road into the forest, into the unknown, with its mysterious marine fog and the fall of night. True, he nearly fell off a cliff, but everything turned out O.K. in the end. After a few mishaps, everything turned out fine.

Everything will turn out fine. Surely, everything will turn out fine.

1978: 'Reverend Jim Jones shoots himself in the head and his followers drink or inject Kool Aid laced with cyanide. The mass suicide takes place in the jungle in Guyana.

1979: Akio Morita, Sony's chairman devises a portable cassette player with headphones, called the *Walkman*, so that his children can listen to loud rock music without disturbing him.

THE LOVE SICK BLUES

I was disappointed, my plan hadn't worked, but then I was unaware that being fired would not have qualified a person for unemployment. I continued to go to work but only in guy clothes. I smoked pot a couple of times with Edem Vaz, the Brazilian straight guy at the Bachelors Quarters. An uneventful month went by and I still felt trapped. At least I had an outlandish day at work to add to my repertoire of memories. One morning I got up to piss and the urine was the color of Coca-Cola. Harry, the building manager, was in the kitchen when I came down for breakfast, so I mentioned to him how dark my piss was and he insisted that I should go see the doctor, it could be hepatitis. I went to the doctor that day and it was confirmed; hepatitis. Stay at home for a few weeks and no drinking alcohol. The thought of no alcohol sounded pretty grim, but on the way home on the bus I realized that I had a legitimate reason to not go to work. This already sounded pretty good. I might actually play the keyboard and start composing music again.

I sat down to play music a few times. What I hadn't known about hepatitis is how drained a person could feel. Food pretty much lost its appeal. I think I lived on chicken broth and soda crackers and even coffee gave way to iced tea and Seven-Up. Smoking pot was no fun at all. I'd smoke a little, think a little, look out the window a little, and then I'd lie down.

I did collect disability checks and the whole ordeal lasted about a month. On the third week the doctor said I could start going for walks now. Sorry, still no alcohol.

Coincidentally, on the first day that I managed to go for a walk, the Municipal Bus System was on strike. I went for about a two mile walk across town and ended up calling a bar acquaintance near the Castro. He was handsome enough to befriend, but we were not in love or anything romantic. When I left his house to return home I had no desire to walk, so I stuck out my thumb on Market Street. During my walk from his house, I kept thinking I'm going to meet someone special today. Something unusual is going to happen. The thought ran through my mind enough times that I wondered if I was trying to talk myself into it, or what? You know, like the power of positive thinking, or just a premonition. I wasn't sure. It was probably just the inklings of hope that would come to nothing, I thought.

Finally, an old rusty beat up pickup truck pulled over. I wondered at the dinginess of the driver if some farmer was passing through town. It would take a small-town type to have the old-fashioned hospitality to pull over for a hitch-hiker. He said he needed to stop for gas, but he could drive me home. He had a curly mop of hair like Bob Dylan and an unkempt beard. His name was Johnny. It was raining now and getting dark. I told him I liked how the city lights reflected in the asphalt and he said yeah, he wished he were on L.S.D. I let out a comfortable laugh to show no sign of disapproval at the mention of drugs. (Maybe this guy is the stoner type that lives out in the boonies.) He dropped me off right at the black door that said Bachelor's Quarters. I thanked him and went up to my room. Ten minutes later there was a knock on the door to tell me I had a phone call. I went downstairs to the payphone, and it was Johnny, asking where I was from and saying it must have took a lot of nerve to just move out to San Francisco with two hundred dollars, not knowing anyone. I told him about my job and my electric piano and he told me about his little house, well really not so little, and he was putting bubble wrap on the windows for soundproofing. He told me how egg cartons worked great to soundproof a room for musicians rehearsing or recording. He said he lived in a household of vegetarians and he wanted to invite me over for dinner. When he found out that I was recovering from hepatitis he said the best thing for the liver is carrot juice. He had a juicer and he'd make me some carrot juice.

I was over at his house the next day, eating spinach salad with nutritional yeast. And the carrot juice was so sweet and divine. It didn't take long for him to scheme up a plan that I could stay in his room mates' room until they returned from vacation. One day I got in his large bed with him. He had put on Brain Eno's Discreet Music. The album is a creation of tape loops and it had a mesmerizing tranquilizing effect. This was the calming music that convinced me that my life had now changed.

I ended up moving in with Johnny. From upper Market Street the house looked like a little Snoopy dog house with a garage door, but upper Market is a road that curves up a steep San Francisco hill that overlooks the city, and the rest of the house sprawls out below the street level, two and three floors down. There's a sunken living room with curtains that open onto treetops that slice a panorama of the city and sailboats on the bay far off and below, like some view from an Italian villa.

Johnny was a hardcore dumpster diver. The whole house was done in deco-wrecko. He also believed in recycling cans and plastic and newspapers and he wanted to put in solar energy modules. He had an Ionizer in the living room. If you put your nose up to it there is a smell like fresh air before a rainstorm. He had an unusual creation made of a glass case on a wooden stand. Inside were collector light bulbs with neon flowers and angels inside them. The light bulbs were circuited to the equalizer of his sound system so that the lights would dance on and off according to the bass, midrange, and treble of the music being played. This memory of his homemade lightshow perfectly depicts the delicate genius of Johnny at his best. During one of his depressions, he watched television endlessly with a cord that stretched across the room to a foot button that turned the sound off and back on. He called it a commercial canner. But for all the inspiration and charm that Johnny could surround you with, there was an equally dark and sinister and envious, vindictive side. He was manic-depressive and both ends of the wide spectrum could become unbearable. He knew all about lithium and refused to take it. We all suffered, and boy did he know how to suffer.

He introduced me to the *Guardians of Sunlight*, a local theater group. Most of the participants were vegetarian. There were some horrifying shows that I endured in the late seventies, but talent and practice, practice, practice lead to a polish and cohesiveness in performances that made some of the early eighties shows more intriguing and clever with moments of truly memorable inspiration. By that time I had separated from Johnny, but we remained friends especially with our creative links in music and performing.

Johnny had a verbally hateful relationship with his mother. I couldn't believe the insults and bad mouthing he would resort to, talking to her on the phone to New York. Johnny was from New York. I never heard her voice personally, but he told me that she said horrible demeaning things to him: You worthless piece of shit. He was about thirteen years older than me and pretty beaten down from drug abuse. He warned me to stay away from amphetamines and he also told me about the endless black crud that he coughed up when he quit smoking cigarettes. He could not tolerate cigarette smoke or smokers. But amphetamine, or speed, was the worst, evil, demonic and ruinous drug anyone could get involved with. I never asked for his opinion on heroin.

I'm now convinced that our relationship was poorly defined and therefore lacked mutual agreements and shared expectations. He had suggested we have an open relationship, but probably because I hadn't exactly fallen in love with him and he didn't want to scare me away. We went to the bathhouse together, and it felt a little awkward to look for somebody else when I was already with him. He was a bit of a lunatic, though, so it wasn't difficult emotionally to chase after other guys and feel relieved to spend time with a calmer more stable type. One night I did go to the bathhouse on my own and I met this very handsome guy named Michael who was closer to my age. He was muscular, but not overly so. His face was a very refined, a matured cherub face with large pensive eyes and a soft dark mustache. I invited him home and we really enjoyed each other and I felt truly passionate when we kissed and hugged and caressed and then devoured each other.

We exchanged numbers and the near future found us together many times. The first morning after he left, the whole world looked bright and cheerful to me. Johnny was in the kitchen reading the newspaper. Michael had gone home. When I said Good Morning to Johnny, he grabbed me and threw me across the kitchen. I fell against a chair. I was caught off guard, but not hurt. What's wrong with you? I doubt that I even possessed that much communication skill when the heat was on. I probably glared at him and said Jesus, or just disappeared in my room, grabbed a few things, and left the house quickly.

He had proposed an open relationship and I had taken his word at face value. His violent reaction seemed like a childish tantrum and I had absolutely no experience coping with tantrums. Not in those days.

In the midst of my living with him, he inherited a lump of money. Maybe his dad died. He would never give me a straight explanation of where the money came from. One of his stories was that he mailed some money to Reverend So-and-So back east who always preached the miracles of the lord, and lo and behold, he received a big check in the mail. At any rate, he started purchasing synthesizer keyboards and recording equipment: TEAC tape recorders and equalizers and reverb machines and microphones. I learned that L.E.D. stands for light emitting diode and how to set volumes for recording levels by reading how far the pins were bouncing into the red.

An unspoken competition among his friends was building to get chances to use Johnny's equipment. I was one of the competing friends. Andy and Tanya, the couple back from vacation, kept a piano in the front room and in no time new compositions were springing from my fingertips. Johnny's full size Moog synthesizer stood on metal stand and the variety of settings and adjustability of the sounds were astonishing. I gradually learned to enhance the sound quality and dimension with Johnny's recording devices.

Early in my Upper Market Street days, I completed a piece that I titled *L.F. Ant* because the piece lumbered and built up to a dramatic surge. A recording of the piece with the piano overlaid with synthesizer ended up in a performance called Machine Worship with modern dancers dressed like veiled Ninjas that prostrated themselves to the modern God, the Age of Machines. By merging a fellow musician's recording followed by my *L.F. Ant*, the Machine Worship dance was a haunting and gripping performance. We added drum trills and the percussion built to the grand finale that landed on a Chinese gong.

Audience response ranged from excitement to goose bumps. One spectator claimed later that the piece had given him nightmares. I had loved as a teenager the soundtracks of Bernard Hermann created for Alfred Hitchcock movies. My favorite was his music for *Vertigo*. I also learned in San Francisco to enjoy Nina Rota's scores for Fellini, so I was later able to recognize these influences when Danny Elfman made it big with *Pee Wee's Big Adventure, Edward Scissorhands, Bat Man* and even later *The Simpsons*. These were my music idols, along with the folk to jazz poetess, Joni Mitchell, the innovative Beatles, the delicate and romantic pieces by Debussy, and the mournful tearful ones of Mahler.

In the midst of my quest for the off-the-beaten-path inspiration and the grandiosity that I aimed for, Johnny started working with a young kid who sang and played Country standards on keyboard. His repertoire included nothing original. Danny Page was little and very cute with his long curly blond hair. He had talent alright. He could sing on key and he played keyboard proficiently. I had to admit that even I was attracted to his charming and gentle nature, but I quickly grew to hate the old worn out tunes. The one song that stuck in my mind was *The Love Sick Blues* by Hank Williams. Johnny was giving the kid a lot of attention and lots of time on the synthesizer and I was envious. I fought my jealousy, I denied it at first. I acted coldly civilized around the two of them while inside I was steaming at the thought that Johnny would push me aside along with my aspirations. I had been replaced by this cutesy little schmuck.

I remember one night I was lying on the couch in the sunken living room that overlooked the city. Johnny was downstairs with Danny either working on music or doing who-knows-what. Maybe something I wish I was doing in either case. There was a pounding sound like the throb of helicopters or bare stomping feet across a wooden floor that came through the house and moved through the living room. I must have been too exhausted or too stoned. There was nothing to be seen making the noise. Somehow to me, that sound was the drum call to war, the cry to battle, the warning that said to me – get out, leave all this behind. That sound stayed with me as a memory of my heartache and the anger that initiated action.

STUCK OUT MY THUMB

It wasn't long after the battle cry pounding that I sat alone at the rehearsal studio at 333 Valencia. The *Guardians of Sunlight* rehearsed in a rented studio that had a loft and a bathroom in the back, probably once a little family owned store. Johnny had set up recording equipment on a roll cart at the side of the room. I had the headphones on and I adjusted the equalizer to run a recording of my music from reel-to-reel onto cassette. Johnny appeared at the door from the street, and I continued my adjustments. He walked up behind me, grabbed my hair, pulled off the headphones and pulled me over backward in the chair. I didn't really fall to the floor. I somehow caught my balance. Maybe I did a summersault. I felt furious and under attack. (No shit, Sherlock!) I *was* under attack.

Johnny was smiling his sinister smile, as if making me angry was his dream, come true. There was a pipe lying on the floor, it was probably the stem for a bicycle seat. I grabbed it and came at him and managed to chase him out the door and lock the door. Within a half a minute, as I searched my alternatives, Johnny started climbing in the open slant window that let in air above the door. I banged at the door frame and the top of the door with the pipe near his fingers and he jumped down and I closed the window.

Several minutes later, the police arrived, and having talked first to Johnny outside, they took me away in their police car. I thought I was on my way to jail. The police and I had a small discussion about what happened from my perspective. Within a few blocks, one of the two policemen commented that lover's quarrels can get way out of hand. He advised me to let things cool off and stay away from each him for a while until we are able to talk without fists and weapons in our hands. They let me out on the curb.

When I went home, Johnny acted like nothing had happened and wanted to hug me. I wouldn't let him and I ran out of the house and down the street. He followed me in his little sports car, a *Karmann Ghia*. He would stop alongside me on the sidewalk and say, "Come on, get in the car, don't be silly."

I remember hiding behind bushes and jumping fences and lying on my stomach, not only to hide from Johnny, but to not be noticed by the owners of these front yards from their houses.

Eventually that same day, I went home, grabbed my little stash of cash that I hid in a box of paperwork, got on a Greyhound bus, and headed north. The amount I was willing to spend landed me in a pitiful little town where I knew I couldn't stay, so I walked a little further up the highway with my sleeping roll and suitcase, and stuck out my thumb. Nobody pulled over for about forty-five minutes and dark was setting in, so I gave up on traveling for the night, hopped the wooden fence of a big field of tall grass, and slept there in the grass of a field near the road.

THE ANGER BOX

Rajah awoke in the expanse of Jacob's brass bed. The curtains were drawn and the lamp was off. The room was soft and dark. Rajah could see the jagged glow of daylight on the carpet where the curtains touched the ground. He put on his underwear and opened the curtain. He sat on the bed's edge in a drowsy daze. Jacob had received a phone call from the travel agency and told Rajah to stay and take a nap until he returned.

On the nightstand sat the old fashioned rotary-dial phone, a clay-caste Buddha, and a redwood jewelry box. Almost unconsciously, Rajah lifted the lid to the jewelry box. Silver cufflinks, a skeleton key, Egyptian pounds, folded, and a hatpin with a ruby on it were the contents. Rajah gently closed the lid and his mind pictured a red envelope beneath the jewelry. Just to check if his mind was playing tricks, he opened the box again. Yes, there was a red envelope, (none of his business). He closed the lid again. His mind pictured himself opening the envelope and he couldn't resist. He dumped the contents of the wooden box onto the pillow and pulled out the envelope. It wasn't sealed. Inside was a letter, handwritten.

January 8, 1974

Dear Jacob,

I'm sorry that I left without saying goodbye.
I hate to tell you this by letter but I will not be
returning. I do no hate you. I have tried to tolerate
your anger and judgments without retaliation.
Before meeting you, I spent five years learning to
accept and love my life and the human race. It's not
easy, but I have to practice God consciousness to stay
away from alcohol and drugs. Anger and judging
others are part of my disease.

I know that you have stopped using drugs for over
a year now, but your anger and negativity is wearing
me out. It is too much my own nature to look for the

bad in people and situations and spend too much time in frustration.

I cannot afford to do this. I need to fill myself with affirmations and forgiveness. God knows, I am far from perfect, and it is unfair for me to expect other people to have no flaws.

I have tried to accept your flaws and hold onto my own positive outlook. Unfortunately, your negative and demeaning comments are so frequent that I feel saturated, overwhelmed, and drowning in your perspective. You are not a bad person. You are not evil. You are only following poor examples.

I need a serious break from your outbreaks and cutting comments. I try to feel close to you, to be supportive, but it feels like there is a thick curtain around you, an iron curtain, so to speak. The curtain is your anger. You hate this, you can't stand that. You keep pushing the world and everyone away from you, including me. You refuse to take advice. I would tell you to draw back the curtain, to set aside your hate and judgment, to look at me and the rest of the world without so much rage and criticism. You are hurting yourself the most.

If I thought you would listen I would make you an Anger Box. There would be a slit on top like a piggy bank where you could slip pieces of paper into the box. Whenever you hate something or criticize someone, you would write it on a piece of paper and slip it into the box. Once it's in the box, you can't take it out. You can no longer repeat that comment. It stays locked up in the box and you never say it out loud. Comments like this;
    I hate this signal light, it always turns red when I get here.
    Look how fat and ugly that woman is!
    You're an idiot. Thirty years old and you're still

an idiot.

    I hate it when my mother says that.

    She looks horrible, she has no class.

    Why do they always have to be so rude?

    God hates me.

    That's stupid. What do you expect from somebody with no education?

You would put all these comments away in a box. Learn to stop talking like this. These judgments and criticisms and expressions of anger are repeated and repeated like exercises in a workbook. They have become your mantra, your chant, your ongoing prayer. You are teaching yourself that everything sucks, that you will always be a loser, and everyone else is doing everything all wrong. Stop talking yourself into bad news. You're talking yourself into a bad mood.

Draw back the heavy curtain of anger and judgment that surrounds you and look at the world without all the darkness you put upon it. If you can turn into a drug addict, then you're not perfect. How can you expect everyone else to be perfect? Do you really think that you know better than God how people should behave and dress and eat and perform and treat you? Maybe they're just doing the best that they know how, just like you and me. Take all of that dead weight off your shoulders and just accept things the way they are.

It's OK if I want to make a change for the better. Most likely, the changes I need to make are in myself, and I'd do better to keep my nose out of other people's business. To me, God is about love, not hate. God is about tolerance, not criticism. You know, I could look for what a person is doing right and encourage him. Why would I choose to be miserable? Why do you?

Jacob, I still love you. You are not a loser. You have many outstanding and inspiring qualities. I am

leaving your anger and hate, not you. Please know
that I value all that we have shared.

                              Goodbye with love,
                              Phillip

    Rajah puts back the letter and the contents of the jewelry box.
1974? That was nearly ten years ago. Maybe Rajah doesn't
know Jacob very well after all.   Jacob's nightmares and night
terrors seem so unrelated to Jacob's personality, but anger and
hate? Rajah hasn't seen this side of Jacob yet. Maybe the living
room décor is more revealing than Rajah perceived.

I made it through the long line. My double espresso is being drawn, but there's an interruption. Oh well, I'll read the horoscope. SCORPIO (Oct. 24-Nov. 21)   Opportunities are never lost. The ones you miss will be taken by somebody else. This morning, be on your toes for opportunities. Tonight, spend time with an acquaintance, somebody who has good influence over you.

That's what it says. Someone will take the opportunity I miss. I didn't do the dishes yet and nobody took that opportunity. Keep on my toes? Should I be testing the floor planks in the café for a hidden stash of cash? Maybe I should step out onto the sidewalk and bump into the man of my life, a real dreamboat. I stand outside the door for about three minutes. No dreamboats here, all I see are shipwrecks. It also suggested that I spend some time tonight with someone who has good influence over me. Am I expected to rely on my primitive judgment as to who this "good influence" will be? Usually the ones who are a good influence are the ones I find irritating.

The newspaper and magazine horoscopes can be a big letdown. The odds are one in twelve that they might tell me about myself. Many moons ago, a friend did my chart for me. He was a cute little guy who loved football and knew astrology in depth. I found the information remarkable. Even for a disbeliever, the probing of an individual's character and his attributes are fascinating. The reoccurring coincidences lead me to seriously wonder. If the tide can be pulled by the moon, why wouldn't our personalities, likewise, be pulled by the planets? It doesn't sound plausible to me, but I have had so many Cancer roommates and Cancer coworkers who are natural friends, frequent close friendships with Pisces people, and other Scorpios seem to make the most sense of all human beings to me (I'm a Scorpio). These three signs are the water signs. Water mixes well with water. Mix a water sign with air and you get bubbles. Mix water with a fire sign and you get steam. Mix water with an earth sign and you get mud.

It is said that Scorpio is ruled by the planet Pluto, the ninth and usually the farthest planet from the sun. It takes about 248.4 years for Pluto to complete its revolution around the sun. It travels far, not necessarily at a slow velocity, but two and a half centuries is a long journey compared to other planets. Plutonium was named after this planet. Plutonium is a radioactive metallic element occurring in uranium ores. A scorpion is poisonous, and so is plutonium. Pluto is also a god from Roman mythology. The Roman Pluto is god of the dead and ruler of the underworld. Is it a coincidence that Halloween is celebrated on October 31st during the sign of Scorpio along with the Mexican Day of the Dead celebration also on a Scorpion day at the beginning of November?

After looking at my chart, my cute little friend who loved football looked back at my elfish face. Apparently, he didn't see in me a deadly poison person who ruled the underworld. He told me that the ancient Scorpio was ruled by the planet Mars because the far off Pluto had not yet been discovered with a telescope. He said that there are dark Scorpios and light Scorpios. The ancient symbol, the scorpion (a crustacean like the crab) resembles the dark Scorpios. Of course, dark Scorpios populate the modern world. A more contemporary symbol for Scorpio is the Phoenix, the bird from Egyptian mythology. This mythical bird lived in the desert for 500 years, was consumed in fire, and then rose from the ashes, renewed. There's another version of the story; the Phoenix that flies higher and higher, up to the sun, where it is also consumed in fire. Depending on the Scorpio you meet, or what time of the month it is for this Scorpio, you could be meeting a treacherous and extremely vindictive person, or one of high ideals who lives with honor, honesty, and high integrity. Just like the planet's two-and-a-half-century long revolution around the sun, a Scorpio may be slow to respond (he seeks precision and clearness in his words) he may lag behind and keep you waiting, but his endurance is incredible. The hare may run faster than the tortoise, but guess who wins the race! The slow enduring one can be relied upon to cross the finish line.

Slow, plodding, but enduring is a good description of me and my personal taste. When I was only fifteen, I went with two high school friends in Utah to a Symphony Concert at the local junior high school. For young people, I am sure that the director picked out some playful and energetic pieces, so as not to lose his audience. He did, however, pick a very slow paced and emotional piece; the *Adagietto from Symphony No. 5* by Gustav

Mahler. Some of the individual notes and chords of this piece seem to hang suspended in the air for twenty to thirty seconds. There are moments of clashing dissonance as the mood shifts from heart felt loss to desperation and back to small rays of hope. I wouldn't know if it was a lover's broken heart or a mother's loss of child, but halfway through the piece, the tears rolled down my face and onto my shirt. I may have been a morose teenage, and Lord knows the world has seen and still sees many, but I was also a Scorpio, and this music was not the hectic pace of Mercury zooming around the sun at an incredible pace to keep from falling into the blazing fire. It was the language of Scorpio, slow and deliberate, emotional, enduring, and moving.

My cute little football loving friend was a Cancer. He pointed out that both Cancer and Scorpio may be hard on the outside, but soft on the inside. It all made so much sense to me.

Jacob would wake up at various hours during the night, sometimes screaming, sometimes yelling, "Mama! Mama!" and other times, without waking, would carry on a conversation with who-knows-who in his dream or nightmare. Rajah was put through endless unexplained abuse in the middle of the night during Jacob's unpredictable nightmares; being accused of cheating on Jacob, being shoved out of bed onto the floor, or being spitefully told, "Do not touch me, get away." One night Rajah awoke to Jacob's yelling, "Why don't you just leave, asshole?" This was one of Rajah's earlier visits to Jacob's opulent bungalow, and Rajah got up and went to the living room to sleep on the couch. The living room was decorated as a jungle, with rubber trees, a zebra made of granite, and a tall ceramic giraffe whose silhouette overlooked the couch where Rajah chose to lie down. The living room's daytime charm had turned ominous and threatening in the night. By morning Jacob always forgot his nocturnal tantrums and that particular morning he wondered why Rajah was on the couch. Jacob was brewing espresso, buttering toast, and whistling like a morning lark as if nothing had happened.

Rajah quickly learned to expect no less than Mr. Hyde in the middle of the night with Jacob, although there were unexpected dialogues that ended on a much lighter note. One night about three a.m. Rajah woke up to Jacob's mumbling, "You need to telephone them also, because you have a credit card too." He adds, after a slight pause, "I bought some bananas for your cereal." Rajah asked, "Are they real bananas or dream bananas?"

The following night Jacob's dialogue woke Rajah up again. "I just had a baby, it's a boy. I love babies."

Rajah learned to take the dream behaviors with a grain of salt. The voices and statements emitted from Jacob's mouth in the dead of night were as significant as a television that came on by accident. The voice was directed at the players inside Jacob's head, and not at Rajah, beside him in bed.

They grew attached to each other. They became secret lovers. Perhaps it would not have alarmed Germaine to know that her son had found sexual intimacy with an older man, but

Rajah's new family in Cairo would surely mock him, scold him, and disown him. Particularly dangerous was his stepbrother Qassem who had opened the world of the coffeehouse to begin with. Qassem not only had a hawk eye out for beautiful females, he was very inquisitive. "What are the girls in France like?......Do you find Egyptian girls beautiful?......Would you like me to introduce you to this young lady buying palm dates?.....Have you ever kissed a girl?.....Are you crazy or are you just shy?"

Qassem's playfulness might have easily turned malicious if he were to discover Rajah's secret life. Qassem more easily than anyone else would be the leak in the dike that would expose Rajah to everyone. Now Rajah began to learn the life of the double agent. At home (and at Khunfi's first wife's home) Rajah was innocent and obedient, awaiting the fated future that included a wife and children and obligations. On his getaways with Jacob he lived his underground life, the life he must carefully disguise to others.

Germaine sensed that Rajah had discovered the sensual rewards that come with adulthood. She would ask in vague unconcerned tones, "Where have you been all night, my little Romeo?" His various lies about studying with classmates or outings with Qassem were not skillfully designed, but Germaine believed strongly in freedom and liberty in a very liberal way. Her philosophy matched her past, her lost life as a nomadic hippie love child. She now blamed drug abuse for the fragile health she now endured, but she also blamed the rigid lifestyle of the people who surrounded her for dousing the passionate flame of a free spirit. She became a recluse. Her energy ran low and she spent whole mornings or afternoons sleeping. The books that she attempted to read fell frequently to the floor as she dozed off on the couch. She tended house only on the occasions of Khunfi's return from long business trips. Soon, housekeepers were hired to clean while Germaine went for walks or slept in her room where sunlight was rarely allowed. Food and caffeine replaced her old addictions. She gained weight and new clothes were always a necessity for keeping up with her enlarging size. Early during her gain in pounds, she would spend endless amounts of time in front of the mirror, masking her haggard face in face paint and eyeliner. She covered the new bulges in her thighs and hips under Egyptian robes or loose garments. Her flesh sagged listlessly and she soon learned to avoid all reflections and mirrors while undressing or bathing.

Her complaints to Khunfi about her weight gain were silenced by his endearing quips. "I love a woman who loves to eat." "Now there is more of you to love." "I used to fantasize about making love to large women, and you are fulfilling my fantasies."

In the mid-eighties I began to unravel. I stayed rent free one summer in a back room of an old Victorian house near Market Street and Fell. It was a block away from the Palms Café, a trendy glass exterior hangout for punks and deadbeats and a few yuppies in business attire. The old house where I stayed was taken over by Johnny, who had repaired the rain leaking roof for an elderly woman named Elma who lived there alone during the repair job. Soon after the repairs, Elma passed away and Johnny took up rent free residence in the house.

I had seen the old lady a few times at the Palms Café. Elma was partially toothless and dressed haphazard enough to pass for homeless. Her husband had long since passed away, leaving her alone. When rain water started pouring into her bedroom, she moved into her garage downstairs. She had an old black dog. The dog looked like a cross between a black Labrador and a collie. She and her dog slept in the garage on a pile of dirty laundry, and the entire garage was strewn with piles of wadded newspaper that the poor dog had used to relieve himself because Elma rarely took him out for walks. Johnny said that the stench was horrid. He cleaned up the garage for her, took the dog for walks and fixed the roof. He was excited to find out that she was a vegetarian and started making special meals for her.

After Elma passed away, Johnny moved into the house. There were no relatives to be found, so he took over. By the time I moved in, I had given up my job for the school district because cleaning houses was better for my frequently necessary midday drinking habit. Beer wasn't calming the nerves like it used to and I was often seen with a large mayonnaise jar of iced vodka. In the rent free house hold there was another musician friend of Johnny's named Corey. Corey was handsome and quite diplomatic. He had a mop of hair that looked like a Tina Turner wig of those days. His shock of hair didn't appear comical; it coordinated with his rock-and-roll-guitar-player look. Corey had a raspy deep voice and his style was reminiscent of Jimi Hendrix. He'd answer the door and yell upstairs, Shawn, get your ass down here. I'd yell back, what about the rest of me? Corey had warned me that I would have to stop drinking altogether. His mother was an alcoholic and had finally stopped. He said that without alcohol I would have a lot more energy. This was one of the first opinions that I trusted, but later on, during the early years of my sobriety I wondered, where is all this energy he told me I would have? He lied about that part.

I still owned a lot of recording equipment and instruments, and about eight years worth of funky clothes, so I had weekend yard sales out on Market Street and I designed a very sheik hat made of deep blue plastic strips, Mylar strips and see through plastic. It looked like a huge splash of water on my head so I tilted it to the side to be extra stylish, hoping to catch attention and lure in more sidewalk shoppers. It's beyond all logic and reason the junk people will buy, but I should talk because it was all my belongings. I'd stand out there with quarts of beer in brown bags and corn chips and within a few hours I was bound to make thirty or forty dollars.

A young lover named Andy no longer lived with me. We had recorded lots of decent music together, but the drugs and alcohol got way out of control. I'd see him occasionally at one of my yard sales or he'd pop by our rent free house and listen to songs that Corey and I were creating. One summer night as I walked out the front door with Andy there were two cats screaming and growling at each other. One would suddenly tear off down the street and I felt as if the cats were only symbolic of something in the air, the end of my relationship with Andy perhaps. The nights of summer in San Francisco can often be foggy and chilly, and the fog would seem romantic or eerie or depressing depending on the mood I was in. Andy said goodbye that night and I felt particularly disturbed, lonely, and disillusioned so I went to a secluded hill that I had recently discovered. The pathway started from behind a school yard and led up through manzanita shrubs and tall fennel plants. The dirt path opened up to a large steep hill with jagged rocks at the crest, and dead yellow grass along the incline. In a small hideaway cove I discovered a small tree that formed a bulbous umbrella with its branches and leaves. I didn't really know anything about prayer or believe in saying prayers for that matter, but this little cove had a rare and quiet feeling to it. I thought perhaps a Native American could be buried here. I knelt down beneath the tree and I found a smooth green egg-shaped rock. I thought of the rock as being a moon rock because I found it in the moonlit evening at this private place. I've kept this moon rock to this very day, years later. I climbed up to the jagged rocks, where a view of the city lights in the fog was spectacular.

Returning to this hill frequently that summer, I also found that crossing over the hill and descending the backside a cluster of pine trees that invited me to climb. The branches were thick and sturdy and sticky with sap. These trees were not shaped like Christmas trees. They fanned out in think branches partway up the trunks and I found one that was climbable to a view of the city from its top. One of the topmost branches forked out in three directions and made a reasonable seat. I could imagine an eagle building its nest there. The wind would move the branches back and forth and the swaying felt dangerous but I learned to trust it. This dynamic hiding place seemed to offer me a bit of power at a time when my life was crumbling both around me and inside me.

It was perhaps 1985 or '86 and in the world news there was mention of an astrological alignment of the planets that was being called the Harmonic Convergence. Gurus and their followers had picked secluded high altitude places to receive the first morning light of a particular day on the calendar believed to be especially insightful for mystics and spiritual leaders and their followers. Many people laughed it all off as left-over riffraff from the overly idealistic sixties, but I felt a longing or at least a true hope that the human race might make a turn for the better. As it turned out for me, I ended up staying awake all night on crystal meth and probably drank a few beers on my way to my private eagle's nest. There I was in the treetop, the sun rising, and I was hoping for a miracle. Maybe I would be a chosen one by the placement of the stars that morning. Who knows? That particular morning, however, turned out to hold no flash of light or visionary revelation for me. Even today, though, I have to give myself credit for trying, for seeking. The Harmonic Convergence, as it turned out, came shortly before the end of my San Francisco story. The very end, for me, of the city of black sheep came the day I rode on a Greyhound Bus from a Salvation Army detox to a recovery home in San Jose.

ONE THING

Still morning sparkles with ice cream truck songs.
A lime tree of sparrows flies off loop-to-loop,
through trees full of coins and small silver fish
that make spidery arches across the wide street.

Clothes lines of tee-shirts and billowing sheets,
of shirts and thick sweaters, silk scarves and gym socks;
stardust and moon rocks, and whirlpools and winds,
a Milky Way turns so gently inside me.

Let go of the one thing.
Please, don't confine me.
I've got these walls inside me
to tear down, brick by brick.

Orange pink clouds crawl on sleepy-head trees.
Two herons wade in the still, wind touched stream.
My shell falls aside me, it wobbles and cracks,
and two eyes look out, not knowing, but trusting.

Soft sunny shoulders of long cabin tables,
our sour frustration wrung out into sweetness,
like lemons that wait to be lemonade,
the slender boy smiles at me in the swimming pool.

Let go of the one thing.
Please don't define me.
I've got enough walls inside me
to keep me being one thing.

FIRST IN FRANCE, NOW IN CAIRO

It was early morning, a school day in March. Rajah had spent the night with Jacob, who fed him breakfast; toast and pouched eggs with crispy bacon. They took a taxi early that morning to the coffeehouse where they had met. Jacob read the paper and Rajah watched the clientele of the café. After coffee, Jacob departed for his job at the travel agency and Rajah went home to change clothes before classes. The apartment was quiet as usual, Germaine always slept in late. Rajah brushed his teeth and combed his hair. He went to the small kitchen for a snack. He found an apple and noticed a bulging envelope on the counter with his name written on it. The writing was his mother's; wide loops that slanted elegantly. Inside was a piece of stationary wrapped around a large stack of Egyptian pounds. The money caught Rajah's breath, it was a very hefty sum of money. The letter was short:

> Rajah,
>
> I have to leave here. I am dying. You will understand. I have lost all my spirit and I must flee from this place and my own depression. I cannot force you to leave with me, I know you have found happiness here. Perhaps you will marry soon.
>
> I will always love you, but I am incapable of helping anyone, not even myself. Your grandmother Emelda will help you if you need anything; money, a car, a home. She has a trust fund set up in your name.
>
> You know how to contact her in Grimaud. Please pray for me and forgive me. I know I have been an unpredictable mother, but I am your mother and I am always proud of you, Rajah.
>
> Love always,
>
> Your Mother

He wads up the note and tosses it across the room. Once again his mother has left him, first in France and now in Cairo.

She is insane! She is not a mother, she is a mad woman, always running away looking for something better. Good riddance, Mother! He paces the room and considers skipping school. What is here for me in this awful place? In his mind he sees Jacob's face and thinks of telephoning him at work; no, not now. He'll have to tell Umaima and Qassem. He goes back to the kitchen and retrieves the wadded note from the floor. He smoothes it out on the table and folds it twice to fit in his pants' pocket.

He goes to school that day, but his mind is elsewhere. By lunchtime he decides to leave and he walks to Umaima's house where he shows her the wrinkled note.

"Oh dear, oh dear, she is a very troubled woman. Why didn't she tell me? I am always here for her. Poor Germaine, I hope she's O.K. And you, Rajah, are you alright?"

Rajah looks her directly in the eye with vacant eyes.

"You must be shaken. Do not worry, Rajah, you are like my own son. You always have a home here. You are always welcome in this house."

"Thank you, she left me quite a bit of money. I'll be alright."

He pulls out the stack of Egyptian pounds and Umaima's head rears back with wide eyes. "Goodness! You are a rich man, but I pity you. I could never leave my children like that, she must be in terrible suffering to make such a choice."

That night Rajah shows Jacob the note. Jacob shakes his head and holds Rajah close to him. "I'm so sorry, Rajah. I am truly sorry."

"Why? It's not your fault."

"No. It's not that. It must be painful for you."

"I guess so. I don't really know how I feel: mad at her, sad for her, or glad that she's gone. I think I feel all three!"

"Well, you have me. I am your new family. Don't ever forget that."

"O.K., Jacob, I won't."

ESCAPE ARTIST

The left wing tips downward, nauseously, but gently. Out the peeling Polaroid double-glass porthole; down, down, down below... a brassy glint edged upon the lead colored bay, and all that worn tire rubber on the endless maze of asphalt.

I escape. The maze is far below, shrinking. Nearly three decades ago, I had entered, faltered, whimpered, and groped. With clenched teeth I had maneuvered to the core, fallen through the black hole, tumbled through the Devil's Triangle... and yet here I was, flying away. I had found my way out, or the way out had found me. Escape artist. And now, there below me, the entire delicious deathtrap remained, framed in this little America West peephole at my shoulder.

> Adios, San Jose
> Good riddance, San Francisco
> I'm outa here, Berkeley
> I'm history, ...see ya.

I know every exit from San Jose up the Nimitz freeway past Fremont and the Dumbarton Bridge through the hellish clot of backed up traffic through *Hayweird*, on up the *Nits Wits Freeway* through the grim parts of Oakland where the double decker *Nit Wits* collapsed in '89 (the cars and people flattened like trash in a compactor). Candide would have quoted Doctor Pangloss, "All must be for the best in this best of all possible worlds"

> Fare-thee-well, Johnny
> Bon voyage, Jimmy
> SaiONara, Eddy
> Hasta la vista, Andy
> Good fuckin' bye, Freddie

Apparently, I had a thing for guys with two syllables in their first name.

Belted into my beige seat with my walkman is ready, I browsed all the cheesy air flight magazines. Let the other passengers bet that I'd be listening to Debussy or Nina Rota, or some New Age drift-with-the-crystals cassette. I'd be the type, definitely not the Bruce Springsteen type. Clandestinely, I'm privately listening to Madonna's "*Just Like a Prayer*" from her Immaculate Collection up here in the California clouds.

Hope to God they've got good espresso in New Orleans. Don't ye worry yeself silly Willy, it's the roarin' nineties, and what are those powdery puffy sugary pastries found in the French Quarters? "*Benyays*"? Lord knows how the French would spell them. (How do you look up beignet when you don't know how to spell it in the first place?)

I look over my coffee cup and Calistoga water out the peephole at the orange clouds and a puddle down there called Lake Tahoe. The October landscape unrolls and rolls by, scrolling on and on to Minneapolis, my change-over stop. Just look at Minneapolis - real winters with gray trees that match a sky on the brink of snow! As I exit the accordion covered ramp I see fog puffs of my own breath and the air bites by face and ears. I'm held captive at the airport and the racketeers of food vending know it. I purchase a pickle and a crumpled sandwich priced more like Veal Scaloppini. I could have bought jewelry for the prices on the soda machine.

I take one bite of the pickle and it reminds me of boyfriends, the sweet and sour of them all that lures me in, but after one bite I think; that's enough. The real boyfriends of my life last about one year. That's my usual endurance, after which I leave them on the paper plate; minus one foot, maybe a hand or a nose. Just imagine all those digested boyfriend body parts!

Upon boarding the flight from Minneapolis to New Orleans, I claim a window seat. I'm happy as a clam until a very unbecoming beast takes the seat next to me. He's a diminutive lunatic with pellet eyes and a greased face that looks like overstuffed upholstery. His demeanor of aggressive concentration makes his face look ready to explode from the pressure. He briefly assesses me with the snootiness of a mole, and then arranges his carry-on in a cubbyhole above me. (Not that I like to be judgmental, but I can't control what goes on in my brain.) His deodorant is failing badly. When he falls to his seat there is a whoosh from the cushion, and under his eyebrows are two rimless round glass plates, without which his eyes would disappear like lost dimes in the folds of a leather chair. I dare not smile or greet him for fear of inviting conversation. God, please save me from him breathing in my direction. I can't imagine anything less than miserably sour breath from such an alarming face.

The pilot is talking to us over the intercom. New Orleans awaits us approximately a half-hour from now. The temperature is 42 degrees, the lowest temperature for October in New Orleans since the 1920's. My Halloween costume might not work out – a loin cloth with a feather headdress, moccasins, and face paint. I'll freeze to death. I watch out the window. Down below day-glow orange clouds drift under the sun. Into the clouds we descend as the windows goes white for five to six minutes until through the mist I begin to make out strings of lights below and huge masses of water. We must be over the Gulf of Mexico.

Nicholas meets me at the airport. He has on his Hawaiian shirt, blue jeans and white tennis shoes. His hair is shoulder length. He has a young George Harrison style about him. We take a taxi to the Hilton Hotel. From there a trolley leaves every hour to tour the city. The hotel has a small gym that I use the next morning while Nicholas goes to his seminar about AIDS treatments and new developments. Later that day I go jogging through New Orleans and even with all my efforts to exercise away the pain, my rheumatism continues to clench at my back like alligator teeth. Nicholas returns to the AIDS seminar in the afternoon while I investigate the French Quarters. I have a late lunch at an old fashioned hamburger joint. The place is tiny and gay and campy, like Hamburger Mary's. The cook places the hamburger slabs under a hubcap on the grill, a variation of Pheasant-Under-Glass.

That evening I feel too exhausted and pain ridden to go with Nicholas to check out the bars, but I don't want to be a complete dud. I pretend to have hope that getting out will make me feel better. Lo and behold, I do feel better – for about fifteen minutes. By then Nicholas orders his first gin and tonic. I realize that I need to return to the Hotel and the warmth of the bed. (Getting vertical takes pressure off the spine.) I drink bottled soda water because I haven't touched alcohol for six years. Nicholas, however, does not want to spend all of his New Orleans stay in the hotel. I can't really blame him, so I go back to the hotel alone. He says he'll be back to the hotel room in a little while. I turn up the heat in the room. The bed may be good for my back but not for my brain. The wheels start turning and the squirrel cages are spinning and whirling. I wonder what Nicholas is doing. Who is he talking to? I consider him unusually handsome, and now he's alone in a gay bar. Supposedly, he's still alone. When is he coming back? Does the thought of ME even cross his mind? So forth and so on, *As the World Turns* plays havoc in my poor tired head.

Of course, within an hour and a half, he returns. Immediately he phones a friend in Monterey to check on the status of a fundraising group that donates funds to AIDS assistance programs. The group performs lip-sync drag shows. They hold gay picnics, and other outings, like Gay Night at the roller rink. He talks and laughs on the phone and I lie there like a useless lump. Finally he gets off the phone and I have him all to myself.

....

The next day in New Orleans is similar. By evening we are in a gay bar in the French Quarters again. The lighting is neon-violet and we stand on a narrow walkway with a railing, like a second floor balcony on the inside of the bar that runs along three walls. It's the perfect set-up for looking down like vultures at the bar crowd below. Guys lean on the railing dangling their drinks.

In the boom of music and bar noise, Nicholas is telling me that he's not sure that he wants to live with me in Monterey. I'm a little dumbfounded, because I had just finished moving into his room at Casa Miguel, which is a house for men with AIDS. The house is named after a man who died of the disease. During the three or four months that we were getting to know each other, we lived in separate cities, about an hour and a half apart by car. Lots of phone calls and visiting each other led to my decision to move in with him. I packed my belongings and moved in with him.

Nearly a year before I met Nicholas, I had driven a set of golf clubs from San Francisco airport to Pebble Beach Resort in

Carmel. I had been sitting at San Francisco airport about two a.m., hoping that my work day was just about over, when the dispatcher got the call. It must have been four or five a.m. when I arrived in Pebble Beach. Even in the dark I was overwhelmed by the beauty of the place. Monterey cypresses arched their branches inland, as if the sea breezes were permanent. There were curving roads and unique cottages and dream homes nestled among trees and foliage and flowers. In the daylight there are magnificent views of the ocean.

As I dropped off the golf clubs at the resort I saw more Rolls Royces, Mercedes, Jaguars, and BMWs than I was accustomed to seeing congregated in one place. I had to laugh at the thought of my battered little orange Datsun with its white doors. The sun was up by the time I drove back up the coast through farmland and horse ranches and an American life that I tend to think of as long gone, but all the more breathtaking by its nearness to the sea.

We used walky-talkies on the job in the shuttle vans. The Monterey coast was too far out from the airport shuttle base, and the walky-talky batteries would die-out after about fifteen hours. I called the dispatcher by pay phone to let her know I was heading back. She told me later that she was concerned when I described how unbelievably gorgeous the area was, because she knew I had been up for over thirty hours. It sounded like you were trippin' was the way she described it. Within a few weeks I drove down to Monterey on my day off, went to the visitor's center, bought a couple of local newspapers and began investigating the possibilities of me finding a new job and a new apartment or a room for rent. My findings that day were discouraging and the possibility looked bleak. I had to give myself credit for such a mature approach compared to the day I jumped on a Greyhound Bus to Frisco with only two hundred dollars in '75 or hitch hiking to Eureka to get away from Johnny.

By the time I got to know Nicholas, (who was, by the way, my first three syllable-named boyfriend) I was amazed that I was moving in with a guy I was crazy about, and at the same time, into a city a felt ecstatic about. I even saved up some money from the shuttle job. It took a couple of trips to pack Nicholas's Fiat with most of my belongings. One alternative route to Monterey passes through Salinas, just inland and east of Monterey. Salinas is the "*East of Eden*" that John Steinbeck made so famous in his book that came out in the early fifties. Nicholas had let me borrow his car, and I piled my junk into the trunk and the passenger's seat and the floor. I call by belongings junk without the bat of an eyelash. I'm fully aware what my possessions are worth to other people. I do, however, hold onto endless amounts of cheap things that hold for me a priceless history.

Halloween in New Orleans was far too cold for running around half naked as a Native American warrior. The cold weather brought on my back pain, and by the second night there it looked like we would be repeating the arrangement of me horizontal, in bed, and Nicholas going out bar hopping. Upon envisioning this scenario I concluded, "No way!" This great guy is thinking of dumping me because I'm in pain during what should be a fun time on vacation. I get dressed, went with him barhopping, and ended up sipping his gin and tonics. "If Ibuprofen and Tylenol and lots of exercise refused to kill pain, I might as well add a little of my old cure-all; alcohol." These were my thoughts.

The next day we went to a voodoo shop in the French Quarters. There were lots of mysterious and creepy looking things, none of which fazed me or gave me the least little goose bump. I did, nonetheless, purchase a black crystal that hung on a red leather necklace. Nicholas loved the porcelain masks that run rampant in New Orleans, shop after shop. He selected one mask to give me for my birthday. I can't say that I was drawn to the thing, or that I would have adorned my own home with it, but it was from Nicholas. That much gave the mask a sentimental value to me. It was a gift of mixed messages, though, because I was being told on my birthday that he doubted that he wanted to live with me. Whatever appeal I tried to hold for the gift became contaminated.

We took a steamboat ride on the Mississippi. The boat had a giant water wheel and every detail held an early 1800's feel. There was one anachronism; the computer poker games in one small cabin. We gambled a little cash away there. I stepped up from barely sipping Nicholas's drinks to ordering an anise liqueur of my own, in keeping with the French motif.

Rajah and Jacob spoke to each other mostly in French. Rajah's English was very limited and Jacob's primary language was Portuguese. Jacob had attended universities in London and had traveled to the United States and Canada visiting New York, Toronto, and Niagara Falls. English was valuable for the travel agency, but Rajah had not yet lived where English was dominant. This was about to change.

Rajah practically lived with Jacob now, but there were days when Jacob was difficult to be around. It was Jacob's house and every detail had to be clean and tidy. Clean and tidy was not Rajah's forte, and there were trivial arguments about dirty dishes or clothes left on the floor. Toothpaste left in globs on the bathroom sick was not to be tolerated. When Jacob barked at Rajah, Rajah barked back, "Stop ordering me around, I am not your slave!"

"And this is not your house, and you will have to learn to clean up after yourself."

Rajah learned a new tactic in the battle for power; he would storm out of Jacob's house, slamming the door. He would go to his mother's apartment and ignore Jacob for a whole day. His mother's apartment was still his home, but the discomfort of being there had increased. Before, it was irritating to be around Germaine's weary desperation. Now the absence of Germaine was like a loud silence. The walls and even the furniture seemed oppressive to Rajah. Sleeping there was his only comfortable activity. He had long since given up on studying or eating meals there. It was as if a ghost of loneliness hung in the air and drove Rajah out, and he began to wonder if something about the apartment itself had driven his mother insane and then away.

Khunfis returned two weeks after Germaine's disappearance. Rajah showed him the note. Khunfis sat down while reading it. By the time he set the note down he's already claiming that she will return. "Mark my word," claims Khunfis. Rajah replies, "I hope so," realizing that these words are muttered only to appease Khunfis. Rajah seriously doubts that she will return, but keeps this thought to himself. Khunfis assures Rajah that the apartment remains a home for both of them. "You have your schooling to attend to. As you know, I am away frequently, but I trust you entirely. Rajah, you are a responsible adult. I can rely on you to keep this place orderly. You are a grown man and that means exercising good judgment before inviting anyone here. You must assume full responsibility for your behavior here. Understood?"

"You have nothing to worry about. I never invite anyone here."

"I believe you, Rajah. I think you know that I will tolerate no funny business. Your mother may be gone, but you are not to shame me in my own home. I trust that you will think of your mother before you act irresponsibly."

"Yes, sir." Rajah puts on his best poker face. Although he has no intention of throwing a party or having a wild orgy in this apartment, he wonders what Khunfis refers to by "funny business." What does Khunfis mean when he says "act irresponsibly"? Has Khunfis caught wind of the love affair that Rajah is having with a man? Has Qassem revealed to his own father that Rajah has recently experimented with drugs and alcohol? Perhaps these choice of words refer only to the general knowledge that teenagers have been known to act childishly, but a fear rises in Rajah's throat. He can only hope that his face has not turned red. If his face gives nothing away, perhaps Khunfis really will trust him.

Rajah continued his visits to Umaima's house for the company and the homemade meals. Qassem sensed a new edginess in Rajah and tactfully avoided mentioning the disappearance of Germaine. Qassem became determined to cheer up his friend with the usual girl watching and coffeehouse outings. Rajah rapidly developed a new recklessness around Qassem, forcing himself to smoke the water pipe and making blatant advances on beautiful young women. This change in attitude gave Qassem a sense of accomplishment and added an entertaining diversion to his daily routine. Qassem watched as his pupil tested the waters, and Qassem knew that opportunities came frequently through associates. He had every intention of benefiting from Rajah's acquaintances.

Rajah felt like an actor in a play. His heart was not invested in these adventures, but what was there to lose in trying?

Perhaps he would stumble across a surprising new joy. Why would so many men be so insanely drawn to women and dancing and music and debauchery? There must be something Rajah didn't know, that he had not yet experienced. This rationalization encouraged him to act out upon Qassem's dares. But rationalization was not the core of his motivation toward recklessness. There was a true desire to break away from the Rajah that he had always been, to transform himself into somebody else, somebody less reserved and less accepting. A spirit of rebellion was brewing beneath the surface, a wild man that wanted to knock all the books off the shelf, to disregard ancient laws and make his own laws. A spirit of manhood was surfacing. Germaine's disappearance had sparked this transition that had sat crouched like a cat ready to pounce. Rajah was sixteen. The time was right.

Rajah's escapades with Qassem led to smoking opium and marijuana, and a couple of experiences with hired prostitutes. Rajah felt little inclination to drinking, but one festive night with Qassem, a gentleman bought them each an anisette imported from Greece called *Ouzo*. The drink was odorless and cloudy white over ice. It tasted like licorice candy. Rajah had tasted whiskey and vodka and found them disgusting, but Ouzo seemed innocent and sweet. A second round of drinks led to a third and soon Rajah was extremely drunk. He laughed and fell on the floor and continued to laugh. Qassem dragged his friend out to the alley where they both sat and sang loudly until somebody from a room above dumped water on them.

These outings took their toll on Jacob, who began to worry about losing Rajah entirely. Arguments between them would lead to Rajah's disappearances, followed by apologies, making up and falling in love all over again. Jacob became Rajah's home base. After wild nights and new experiences Rajah always returned to Jacob's bungalow for the compassion that had no strings, and for the sanity of a down to earth life. The intimacy that Rajah shared with Jacob was not induced by a drug or a drink. There was a sincerity about sharing each other and no stage performances were called for. Jacob knew that Rajah was young and needed to explore the possibilities. He missed Rajah when he was gone, and lost sleep wondering what Rajah would find. He mentioned this to Rajah, but he did not hound him. He backed away from laying down heavy laws. He took a chance by letting Rajah run free. His intuition told him that scolding and possessiveness would scare Rajah away permanently. Every time that he opened the door and saw this beautiful young man standing there, he knew that the freedom was a huge gamble. Who wouldn't snag Rajah up, take him away, and keep him in a golden palace? It was very painful to let Rajah go carouse about the streets, but Jacob knew one thing about love; it cannot be forced upon somebody. Nobody can demand that you love someone. Love has to be discovered within oneself. If Rajah wants to return, he must return of his own free will.

These challenging months were like a huge yo-yo to Jacob's heart and spirit. As it turned out, Jacob's gamble paid off. One night, very late, Rajah appeared at Jacob's door. Jacob could see that Rajah was high on some drug and smelled of alcohol. He thought of turning him away in this condition, but the thought of knowing where Rajah was brought a relief that Jacob surrendered to. Jacob demanded that Rajah shower and brush his teeth. That night in bed Rajah confessed to Jacob the true nature of his new habits.

"It starts with a frustration, or a boredom, a claustrophobic feeling, like I can't stand who I am. Why am I here? What am I doing in Cairo of all places? My mother dropped by my grandmother's in France a few years ago, drags me across Italy, meets a man, gets married, and Bingo! Here I am with her in Cairo in that God awful apartment. Then she goes nuts, disappears, and leaves me behind. The whole situation enrages me. And my nosey step-brother Qassem, what a ditz! He always wants to prove what a lady's man he is and I get caught up in his game like some puppet on a string. That's what I feel like; a puppet on a string, dancing this jig to keep everyone entertained. It all came to me tonight. I don't want to be with this pretty lady putting on the moves. I get high and all I can remember is what a mess my mother made of her life. When I lived with my grandmother, I told myself I would never turn out like that. But look at me! This is not me. Some demon that once possessed my mother and drove her crazy has now latched on to me, and wants me to lose my mind, too. I am becoming my mother. I'm following in her doomed footsteps down a path to nowhere. I am just an actor on a stage, and the audience is watching me make a fool of myself. The only place that I can be myself is here with you, Jacob. We may fight and slam doors, but we get over it and make peace again. I don't feel like a fake or a fraud with you. With you I find what is real about myself, and I really do care about you. There is no audience here. I don't have to perform for you."

Rajah kisses Jacob, whose face is dripping with tears.

"Your face is all wet. Jacob, are you crying? Why are you crying?

"I love you, that's why. I love you very much."

THE TELEPHONE LINES WERE DOWN

My life turned from magically in love to dreary and depressed in no time it takes to snap fingers. I found a job in Seaside, just inland from Monterey, working for Costco during the Christmas rush. The store was huge, of course, and I spent the whole day in the parking lot collecting shopping carts. It was an extremely repetitive job, but I found an occasional thrill in stringing large numbers of carts into extra long trains and then maneuvering the heavy beast through the coming-and-going of Christmas shoppers in their vans and pickup trucks, station wagons and sports vehicles. It took a certain amount of courage or foolishness to get up to a running velocity with a long train of carts and then dash ahead of it, to halt it before it crashed into an old lady or somebody's new Lexus.

Costco laid me off the day before Christmas Eve. Merry Christmas and Ho, Ho, Ho. Mark up one more point for the good ol' corporate dollar. I applied for unemployment and discovered that unemployment encouraged classes while collecting benefits. Most of the classes seemed pretty grim: how to become a cashier, a file clerk, or doing grounds maintenance. I'd already done these types of jobs. One class caught my eye, Film Making. A voice inside my head was saying, "Impractical, farfetched, doesn't apply to a real money-making job, and therefore, a waste of time." The invisible entity jabbed me in the ribs as if to say, "Follow your heart, seize the day, go for it!"

I collected the unemployment and took the film making class. In the midst of all this I had become an insomniac and the exhaustion was building up to a severe depression that was sparked by the fact that Nicholas had moved into a ranch house outside of Castroville with his "friend" who he had been calling from New Orleans. They were both very involved in the fundraising Court, a campy, glitzy group that elected a yearly King and Queen. Nicholas and this other guy became a new couple. I knew when I met Nicholas that he had lost his lover to AIDS only six months earlier. I had even discussed with him that it was risky for me to get involved with a guy who had just lost his partner. I had nearly predicted a down fall, but now I had to deal with the reality of my own loss. I thought I had met the perfect guy, and now he had ditched me.

One evening at a memorial ceremony event that was held at a small park off the bay, I spotted a man I had known from San Jose. I told him about the heartbreak I was going through. He drove a red Jaguar and his home was a spectacular two story Spanish style adobe dream house way up on the hill in Pacific Grove above the army base. The Army base took up half of the hillside of rolling grass slopes and pines and eucalyptus trees. If you were to drive over the hill past his stylish house you would arrived in Pebble Beach. He had a spare guest room and rented it to me for exceptionally low rent. Being a nurse, he knew that diphenhydramine hydrochloride not only helps to relieve itch, but makes some people sleepy.

I heard Tori Amos singing on his radio one evening, and purchased a cassette for listening to her on my Walkman as I bicycled across town to my film making class, and then to Casa Miguel to visit the guys I had come to know. Later in the day, I'd bicycle back downtown just below the army base. Downtown was small, but there were a couple of decent espresso cafes. I liked to stop and recharge my internal batteries. (Is that the appropriate New Age terminology?) Tori Amos was the perfect music for my desperate state. A state of shock seemed to fill me up for days and nights on end. I would have to tell myself, "Self, you are not under attack by airplanes that will drop bombs upon your head. This intense fear inside you is really an over-reaction to the innocent and ordinary misfortune that many people have experienced throughout the history of mankind." But these words were like the brain department sending telephone messages to the emotion department at a time when the telephone lines were completely down. The message didn't get through, or else the message did not translate nor did it register as relevant to the emotion department. These horrifying emotions persisted stubbornly, refusing to budge like an obstinate mule: "State of Alarm!, State of Emergency!" they kept insisting like a fire alarm. Maybe my psyche was onto something that my brain hadn't conceived. Maybe my psyche knew that I was in mortal danger. The danger was not a bomb from the sky. The danger was my own self. The state of alarm that I was unconscious of was that I might come to the conclusion that I should kill myself. I had in my lifetime tried suicide at age twelve. I downed a handful of aspirins, which was certainly not a well educated manner of achieving the desired results. I had been through other low points in my life, points when I was capable of sympathizing how a person could resort to suicide.

There certainly do seem to be parts of consciousness that keep themselves in hiding from our own awareness. This is common knowledge: the subconscious and dreams are household terms. How did I get myself locked into a state of shock? Years later it occurred to me to describe this feeling metaphorically – I felt as though I were trapped inside a large lead box that sat on the beach. Inside it was dark and cold and dreary, in fact it was disturbing to realize that I didn't know how to get out. Outside the lead box, people were laughing and playing barefoot in the sand. They were wearing bright colored swimsuits and played with massive beach balls striped with childlike colors. The sky was bright blue and the sun was golden, the sea splashed turquoise, the sand was white and clean. I heard them and I could picture them, care-free and filled with simple joy. I had absolutely no idea how to escape the lead box. I dismally accepted that I was trapped, but a thought came to me. The idea probably was a habit instilled in me during years of Alcoholics Anonymous. The thought was not a habit from my own background. My old self never bothered to expose my own ugly feelings to other people. Why bother anybody with my problems and petty little feelings? Secrecy was my code. Contrary to my old self, what came to me from six years of A.A. was this; I have a voice. Speak out. Tell somebody, anybody. "Hey you out there, you playing with the beach ball! I'm stuck inside this lead box and I don't know how to get out. It's embarrassing to tell you that I'm so stupid that I don't know how to get out, but I need your help. Could you please help me get out of here?"

....

Who did I tell? Believe me, telling anyone that I felt suicidal and had a plan was close to impossible. If I had to walk to the front of a classroom and tell the professor, "I pooped my pants, do you want to see?" I would most likely duck out of the room and say zilch. But there is no toilet that I can secretly go to flush down my feelings of suicide. This was a feeling that sticks inside, and I felt positively certain that one of the last things anybody wanted to hear is a confession of this sort. I had it planned out. I would connect a garden hose to the exhaust of my roommate's car. I would park at a quiet place on the big army base in the dead of night. With the open end of the hose running into the car window, slightly cracked, surely the car would fill up with carbon monoxide.

Shortly before I had become a heartbroken, insomniac wreck, I had set up counseling sessions for myself at Catholic Charities. This was a service offered to people with HIV in Monterey and the sessions were on a sliding scale based on income. My original intention for having the counseling was to help me walk through a fear that was a barrier to my creative success. I can compose and record music, paint pictures, and create films, but going commercial or making a business of my creativity was where I always fell short. Now that I was taking a filmmaking class, and putting my own music to visuals, I would need a counselor to help me walk through my fear: that dreaded step of taking my product out into the public.

On a morning that I was scheduled to see my counselor, a moment of clarity came to me like two pieces of a puzzle fitting together. I have a plan to commit suicide and I'm on my way to see my counselor. Hey! That's the kind of stuff you're supposed to tell a counselor, right? Well, duh! Next he had me telling my doctor and that was another revelation for me. I sat in the doctor's room, on that big fold back chair that has butcher paper over it, waiting for my doctor. It occurred to me that I always think of a doctor as somebody I tell my physical ailments to: this body part hurts or that body part isn't functioning correctly. I don't bring my feelings to the doctor to get cured, but this feeling was pretty severe and the possible outcome would be pretty physical! My thinking **is** part of my body, because my **brain** is part of my body. What a concept! Well, not exactly a lighthearted concept. Actually, insanity is probably a better word for it. Definitely not fun-filled to admit, but the cat was already out of the bag with my counselor anyway. I told my doctor, and I went on to talk to the Catholic Father who founded the AIDS house, Casa Miguel.

The way I'm telling it now, it sounds like I was going around, knocking on doors, telling everybody, "Hey, dude, I've got a suicide plan." But even now, to tell this story, I feel all sticky, like I need to go take a shower and wash this dreadful guck off me. It was a dreadful guck, and every time I approached a person to confess, my logical instinct to clam up would pull on me to not tell. What was the big deal? What was my fear? I can tell you what the fear was. I was afraid that the information would be used against me. Almost anytime that I don't want to let people know that something is wrong with me, (that I'm uncomfortable) or I'm uninformed, or I disagree, or I'm angry or desperate or lost or hurt, my secrecy all boils down to that one fear: I'm afraid the information will be used against me. I'm afraid that some record is being kept, whether it's a mental record or a filing cabinet, the information could be pulled out later and used to my disadvantage.

I found out that I was wrong. After telling three people, they all wanted to help me. I even threw in some extra information; that I was administering alcohol to myself as a last resort pain reliever, and that I had no business touching the stuff, and I should go back to meetings. I signed up for acupuncture, another service that was offered for people with HIV. As I sat one day in the lobby waiting for my acupuncture appointment, my eye caught the title of a book in the room. It read like a saying that stuck in my memory: "When a rosebud is so tightly wound in pain, it has no choice but to bloom." Misquoted or not, the idea has stayed with me. My mother called me in the midst of my glumness (my now confessed glumness) and she said, "Take such good care of yourself that you would be a gift for someone else."

I recently saw the movie "Under the Tuscan Sun" after a co-worker said the story wasn't so great, but the scenery was awesome. A divorcee goes to Italy and discovers the beauty and magic that sill exists in little things, in everything. I cried most of the movie through. To watch her shattered life being reassembled, to watch this soul rediscover the innocence and wonder of all the life that surrounds us; this story resembled my own collapse and the newly found rejuvenation that was to follow. My life would be put back together after being torn apart, and beauty and magic could be found anew.

THE SCRAPBOOK

Rajah bought a notebook with ring clamps and see-through plastic pages for storing papers, photos, ticket, postcards, and personal notes written between Jacob and Rajah. He would color copy the postcards and photos so as to have spare copies for cutting, pasting and creating a collage for the cover. He soon discovered that Jacob would quickly sort through a stack of newly developed photographs and tear up the photos that Jacob considered unbecoming of himself.

"My nose is too fat. I need plastic surgery."

"You can see my receding hairline. My gut is sticking out like a pregnant woman."

Rajah tried to convince Jacob that every photograph held the memory of the moment.

"I wasn't planning to put every photo on the cover of a magazine. My God, you are so self conscious."

"Easy for you to say. You always look like a fashion model."

Rajah did photograph well, but even a photogenic person gets caught from wrong angles and with ridiculous expressions on his face. Rajah showed Jacob a shot that Jacob had taken of Rajah leaning against a wall inside an Egyptian tomb.

"I look deformed in this one, like one leg is shorter than the other."

"You are deformed! Here, let me rip it up."Jacob grabbed the photo, but Rajah wouldn't let go. In the tug of war the photo ripped.

"You're an asshole!"

Jacob just smiled a sarcastic smile.

After nearly a year, the scrapbook was filled with tickets for the trams and busses, photos of Heliopolis, mosques, the Nile, stamps from letters, movie tickets, a small tapestry in bold colors, postcards of the Sphinx, the pyramids, courtyards and festivals, photos of Jacob and Rajah together at the Egyptian Museum, at open markets, aboard various feluccas (the Egyptian sailing boats with their extended lateen rigs). There were stacks of photos and postcards from the Valley of the Kings that Rajah was unable to fit into the scrapbook. He hid these beneath some letters from Grandma Emelda in a shoebox that he hid behind Jacob's skis and fishing poles in Jacob's basement.

WHY AM I HIDING INSIDE MYSELF?

I am not a girl, but I don't think like a guy. You cannot turn me back into a heterosexual man. Likewise, you cannot turn a tangerine back into an orange. Why, if an orange is perfectly tasty, tart, sweet, juicy and healthy, would God bother to make a tangerine? I don't honestly know. Look at cats. Look at dogs. Why so much variety? Beauty is in the eyes of the beholder. Personal taste is in the tongue of the taster. Preference is in the heart of the loved one. Some preferences seem to be in the hormones of the sex drive.

There were no lessons at school to teach me that being homosexual was O.K., or natural or in any way acceptable. There were disdainful remarks from boys at various stages of my development. Who can trust a boy's repulsion? Girls were supposed to have cooties. The dictionary defines a cootie as a slang term for body louse. I didn't know that until I just now looked it up. To me, cooties were some imaginary condition that boys made up as an excuse to feel repulsed. A girl would slime you. She was radioactive and touching her could kill you. It was obviously some vague plague. Boys had the same disdain for effeminate boys. For that matter anything effeminate was plagued. Boys were frequently brutal and drawn to brutality. Torturing cats, smashing turtles, shooting squirrels with bee-bees, beating up other kids on the playground; anything cruel and destructive was a boy's domain. Playing football and joining the military seemed to follow the natural progression; young monsters turn into adult monsters.

Many boys make a fine art of taunting others – *cruelty by words*. "That's dumb, you're a sissy, what an idiot, that's lame, and you're weak. Faggot! Queer! He's gay." These insults were the tip of the iceberg.

It's really no surprise that so many of us learn to hide our true selves. I knew that if I were to say out loud that I hated football, I might as well have said, "Take me to your torture chamber, please." I chose deceit by omission to evade verbal abuse. I didn't think this was lack of confidence so much as I thought it was an intelligent tactic.

Several years after I gave up alcohol and drugs I had a job as an airport shuttle driver. There was a military base near

Redwood City called Moffat Field. It could be seen right off of Highway 101, especially the gigantic hump shaped airplane hanger. On one trip to San Francisco Airport, I had picked up a passenger in Sunnyvale and my second stop was two military men at Moffat Field. The Sunnyvale businessman struck up a conversation with the two young military guys. President Clinton had recently gone into office, and his intended plan for gays being allowed in the military was diminished to the "Don't ask, don't tell," policy. The businessman wanted to know what the military men thought about gays in the military.

Their response was that homosexuals in the military would bring down the morale of the other men. This made absolutely no sense to me, but I kept my mouth sealed shut. I was just the driver. The conversation turned to football. Whose team was going to win such-and-such game and what about so-and-so? I remember feeling mortified that somebody might ask me to comment about football. It bothered me, thinking about this later, that my feathers were so easily ruffled by someone else's opinions and interests.

My roommate at the time said that if he were driving he would have spoken up; "I thought you might like to know that your driver is gay." These words struck me as overly daring, but commendable. I realized, in addition, that I would have to prepare myself for the unavoidable time that somebody asks me about football. I would say, "I don't follow football. It doesn't interest me." These words were honest and at the same time neutral.

Years later, I borrowed a video documentary from the library about the Roman Empire. It contained commentary that supported my distaste for football and boyish or manly brutality. The documentary pointed to the success of the powerful growth of the Roman Empire owing partially to the richness of the Mediterranean resources that Italy possessed. It also pointed out that widespread slavery was a primary resource for the Empire's rise to power. Roman slaves were herded in ropes and chains, whipped, starved, overworked, and punished with severe torture for disobedience. (To my way of thinking, the innocent power trip of a boy who bashes others with his words is merely the seed of a giant power monger who would enslave, torture, abuse, and even kill for personal gain. Personal greed for luxury and abundance has proven itself throughout history as a horrifying drive, a satanic lack of concern for the welfare of others.)

In the video documentary, there were examples shown of the crowds at the Coliseum and the nature of the games played in the arena. Criminals, prisoners of war, and suspected subversives (anyone considered disloyal to the emperor) were likely to be thrown onto the field to battle lions or Roman soldiers. Young boys drawn to brutality would have been in seventh heaven here.

The insight that the narrator of the documentary shared was put simply: The Roman Empire owed much of its success to its army and conquerors of new land. They fought off invaders, collected slaves and ruthlessly enforced command. The average citizen lived a life removed from these soldiers and conquerors. The Coliseum gave citizens a close up display of war with its bloodshed, death, and lack of mercy. This type of entertainment drew the cheering crowd together as fellow Romans against their enemies. Likewise, in the United States, the football stadium is psychologically the same form of entertainment, for the common citizen to experience a taste of war, of his home team squashing the enemy. It seems that man loves the taste of invincibility without compassion like the blood of a lamb in the mouth of a wolf.

Last year, I was especially surprised to see a cover story about football heroes in Sports Illustrated. The cover story, "Play Now, Pay Later," (May 7, 2001) features footballs stars from decades ago, with upsetting photos that display their current lives as older men. There were a variety of gory, disturbing handicaps. Literal lives of suffering were exposed in these stories about football heroes and their permanent handicaps and chronic pain resulting from injuries on the football field.

In the article, titled "The Wrecking Yard," we take a look at Earl Campbell, his arthritic hands, knees and back, now unable to walk more than short distances. Johnny Unitas cannot use his right hand and both of his knees have been replaced. Bill Stanfill keeps his hip bone in a jar, and four of his vertebrae are fused. Harry Carson suffers headaches, loss of memory, and the back of his neck is deformed with bulging disks. Curt Marsh has a replaced hip and his foot is amputated above the ankle. Chris Washington, pictured in a wheelchair, has back spasms, arthritic knees, and as a result of hand tremors, has difficulty holding his baby daughter. I was amazed that Sports Illustrated would cover a story that backed up my repulsion for the game.

My planned words, "I don't follow football. It doesn't interest me," is such a neutral statement. It backs away from stating my loathing for football. My brother once pointed out that some people may find music concerts uninteresting and a waste of time, while others will find football uninspiring. I consider this a very logical statement, a sort of balancing the scales type of insight. That's life. Life goes on. I can't have everything my way. I've learned to face it. Football is not going away and least of all because I'm some pussy-foot pacifist.

Entertainment is in the spirit of the fun seeker, but I still hate brutality. Go ahead. Call me a sissy.

THREADING THE NUMBER 8: INFINITY

I close my eyes and the vines ascend, deep-green and twining, wrapping around Eucalyptus trunks and majestic oaks. The air is cool and vapory, the scent of mud and Vapor-Rub, sweet jasmine, damp roots, and a compost of black leaves. The tangle of stems gives below foot like netting for a trapeze artist beneath my weight in canvas shoes. The oak bark is ridged and cracked, but sturdy to my grip. A ladder of redwood braces, strapped with rungs of thick rope, invites me. Dry strands sting my palms as I climb. I've lifted myself from the vine netting below and ascend cautiously to the high-wire act. I'm surrounded by leaves like giant hands and metallic fish spattered with soft blurs of sunlight. The atmosphere is charged with oxygen. Squeezing myself up through the liver colored slats of a quadrilateral floor; I enter a lofty room, its ceiling too low for standing up. Outside walls of glass are montages of oak, ivy, and sardine shaped leaves.

Two kitchen tables would not fit into this tree house. A chair would not pass through the hole-in-the-floor entrance. On the floor is a deep green rectangular mat, a gym mat, pushed against the wall behind me. I kneel on the mat and close my eyes (the eyes inside my already closed eyes). Inner vision of the subconscious has closed its eyes. Still aware of the glinting glass and wooden space and the rope-rung ladder outside my eyelids; I know, instinctively, that to my left there is a wooden box attached to the wall. This box is mailbox size, its wooden lid angles down from a hinge against the wall. There is no lock on the box's latch. I open the lid, not with my hand, but with my consciousness. I pull out the hammer and bring it (or float it, rather) across the room to where I kneel on the mat and hit myself on the head. My head is not a rock-like skull, not here in this vision. I am gel or smears of light; colors that depict me in prayer.

The hammer pounds into my head, the brain, the thoughts, the spine, and into the space between my shoulder blades – knocking out the clutter of feelings and thought: the gas-and-electric bill, flat tires, car insurance, laundry soap, frustrations, obligations, ...fears. Bang, bang, bang. Out with the anger. Bang, bang. Be gone tense shoulders.   Bang, bang, smash like the sound of shattering glass.

I put back the hammer, levitation style, and pull out a screwdriver from the wooden box on the wall. Time to tighten the third eye (which by now is ready to pop out of my face – bouncing as it hangs from a Jack-in-the-Box spring). The screwdriver floats across the room and tightens the third eye into place. Adjust the hinges of my emotions, while I'm at it. (They do come unhinged, you know.) There's a lump between my heart and throat. Secure this from jumping out of my chest, especially at the mere insinuation of danger; beautiful danger. DANGEROUS BEAUTY.

Gently loosen the tight perceptions, the judgments; by now rusted shut. Rust falls around my feet like paprika snow. I place back the screwdriver in the box. (What is this box? A toolbox?)

The next tool is not ordinary.   I extract (with my consciousness) the sparkler, the wand. The fizzle is potent with healing, well being, safety, protection, faith, and joy (to mention a few).   The fizzling sparkle-powder has settled in the mailbox/toolbox and the sparkler stick has to be dipped and re-dipped like a paintbrush to replenish the fizzle. I push the sparkles into my temples beside each eye; circle my head and my inner-mind. This feels as if I am scraping off old paint. I re-dip the sparkler into the powder and now stripe my neck with sizzling light. Across my shoulders, and then down my spine – encircle my legs with the rejuvenating sparkle. With an oval motion that passes through my heart and genitals, I thread the light though lust and love and the shades of feelings grown in companionship.   Encircle the heart to the brain to the power above me; threading the number 8: Infinity. All three sewn together; the greater spirit, brain, and heart. While I'm at it, I throw in an extra loop to the sex drive for inspirational higher guidance. "Ha," you laugh. I'm serious, I'm telling you. All entwined, now I coil the light from my tailbone up the spinal column until it spirals out the top of my head and back to its source.

Tap the top of my head, once – sptshsh. Place the sparkler/wand back in the wall box. Close the lid. Now I wait. I'm waiting for the arrival of a visitor, a witchdoctor, of sorts, the Healer. He climbs up through the floor entrance looking like a thin rag doll of colored electric wires, yellow, green and white. He places his spindly hands on my brain and pauses at each part he touches as if sending warmth; into my neck and shoulder, my heart, my lower back, and then he brushes his bristling fingertips gently up my spine. He's telling me over and over: "All is well, all is well, all is well……"

THE IMPACT OF A METEOR

I moved from Monterey to San Diego in a powder blue, 1960 Rambler. This old car looked like a children's storybook illustration. It was, however, very heavy. Transmission trouble was a reoccurring episode. I would ride my bike everywhere, while the blue beast sat forlorn on the street until an orange notice would appear on the windshield threatening that the city would be forced to tow my Rambler if I failed to move it. Money to replace the transmission refused to appear for months on end. I kept pushing the car by foot to various nearby streets until the next orange notice would appear.

I lived in a double-deck apartment complex on Park Avenue. One morning a benefactor finally came to the rescue by writing out a check to me to pay for the transmission transplant. This benefactor was a retired army sergeant who had fallen in love with my hunky roommate. "Fallen in lust" may be a more accurate account of the sergeant's condition. At any rate, the love struck man lived upstairs, and he had inherited some bucks. I ended up reaping the benefits of his crush on my roommate. I guess you could have called him my "sugar uncle". There were no feelings of romance between us, thank God.

It took a while to get parts for an old Rambler, believe me. In the morning I had worked at my restaurant job and a co-worker gave me and my bicycle a ride back home. The mechanic left a message on my answering machine (remember those?) that my car was repaired, so I brought the check into the shop. Unfortunately, the check was made out to me. The cashier didn't want to accept a pay-to-the-order, two-party check. I rode my bike to the love-crazed sergeant's bank and cashed the check. On the way back to the mechanic's shop I rode down a side street that had a cement rain gutter crossing the street. The rain gutter made only a medium dip in the road. I noticed, though, that the asphalt along the edge of the gutter had curled up to make a lip about as thick as a boot toe that ran the entire width of the street. I'm no speed demon on my bicycle, but I was excited to get my car. When the front tire hit the asphalt lip, the front wheel came off of the bike. Apparently, I had unloaded my bike from my co-worker's car, and when I put the front wheel back on, I had forgotten to tighten the quick-release wing-nut. The front frame of the bicycle has two tongs that fell dead forward to the asphalt. If I had flipped over the handlebars, I might have broken my arm, or a leg, or heaven forbid, smashed my tailbone. I was going so slow that I fell straight down onto the bike as it slammed the ground. How did that feel? It didn't feel good, to put it in words that won't require censor. It felt like I slammed my head with a two-by-four.

I started bellowing. I let out sounds somewhere between moaning, whimpering and screaming. A woman came out of her house from across the street and a man appeared from the side of the road that I was on. I knew I was supposed to get out of the street before a car turned the corner, but the bike frame was tangled in the bike spokes and I felt stupefied. I seemed to be out of commission. The man told me to sit on the curb. When I sat down I held my head and my hand got all bloody. He said, "Your ear...you ripped most of your ear off." He took off his shirt and told me to press it to the side of my head. "I wouldn't look in the mirror if I were you," he added. I agreed with him entirely. The woman was calling an ambulance.

When the ambulance arrived, the attendant or doctor/nurse, (What do you call a doctor who rides with you in the ambulance?) the ambulance doctor said, "Come on, Van Gogh, we're going to the hospital." At the hospital they put me out with anesthesia and sewed my ear back on with some touches of plastic surgery to make the ear presentable in public.

The next day I woke up in a hospital room. I was in an excellent mood when my roommate arrived with mint-chip ice cream, my favorite. Shortly after downing the ice cream, I was released from the hospital. By the time I arrived home the anesthesia wore off. Boy, did I go through withdrawals! My head was about to explode as I stuck it in the toilet and threw up mint-chip ice cream mixed with bile. (I find it ironical that I can say this without fear of censorship.) My roommate brought me back for a CAT scan, just in case I had a concussion.

I had a plastic bowl on the side of my head, held on with tape wrapped around my head. The doctor gave me a strong pain medication. Later, when I finally drove my car, I felt ridiculous. Usually on the road, there are other cars pulling in front of you or blocking your path with regularity. Now the cars seemed to clear a path just for me, like the parting of the Red Sea. The other drivers must have been thinking, "Look out for that old, beat-up car. The driver has a cereal bowl wrapped to the side of his head in a bandage. There's no telling what he'll do next."

I had two weeks off work to recover. I was free to complete an art project that I had just started. It was a list of names on a big black canvas. The idea came to me one morning when I got up, walked into the living room, looked at my cat, Sweet Pea, bathing herself on the couch, and said, "You think you're the Queen of Sheeba, don't you?" I then asked myself, "Who was the Queen of Sheeba, anyway?" I started making a list of names that have real pizzazz to them. Some of these names, I knew who they were, others, I had no idea, the name simply had a ring to it.

Evel Knievel   Xerxes   Madam X   King Kong

Elvira   Euripides   Dr. Jeckel   Isaac Newton

Helen of Troy   Chubby Checker   Sinbad

I bought from an office supply store a variety of sticky peel-off alphabets in white and red and gold. I chose these colors for the black canvas, thinking of the simplicity of Chinese art. All of the letters were capital, but I bought three different sizes. By making some names big or small or medium I hoped for a three dimensional effect; some names look closer, others look further back because they were smaller.

WILLIAM THE CONQUERER   DR. NO   OL'KING COLE
NEFERTITI   MATA HARI   MR. ED   GERONIMO
BABY JANE   PANCHO VILLA   GENGHIS KHAN
MEDUSA   MARIE ANTIONETTE   FUZZY WUZZY
BILLY THE KID NURSE RATCHET   MARQUIS DE SADE
SUZI WONG   ASTRO PIZARRO BETTY RUBBLE
CATHERINE THE GREAT   FELLINI   LOIS LANE
HOUDINI   GINA LOLLOBRIGIDA   JEZEBEL
JUMPIN' JACK FLASH   ULYSSES   PANDORA
TINKERBELL   NOWHERE MAN   TWEETY BIRD
IVANHOE   GILLIGAN   SNIDLEY   WHIPLASH
AL   CAPONE   LUCIFER   MA   KETTLE

KING SOLOMON   YODA   PRINCE CHARMING
VERUSHKA   SIR LANCELOT   HOWDY DOODY
VOLTAIRE   ARISTOPHANES   LAMBCHOP

I showed the collection-of-names piece at several cafes around town with a caption that read:

LIKE A METEOR

Sometimes a name is very memorable. The sound

alone catches your attention. It's like a meteor,

it has a great impact and leaves a lasting impression.

THREE FROGS ARE GRANTED ONE WISH

One evening, Jacob was sorting through the bedroom closet, deciding what clothes could be given away. Inside a cardboard box he discovered a variety of odd items that belonged to Rajah: a stuffed Pegasus (slightly worn and needing a bath), an ashtray-sized basket, filled with smooth polished rocks, a miniature jewelry box covered with Chinese satin, with an intricately woven floral pattern, containing two heavy yin-yang balls inside. Jacob picked up the yin-yang balls, causing a chiming sound that came from within them. There was a small booklet with a green paper cover and three holes laced with white yarn to hold the pages together. Each page was written by fountain pen. The booklet was a story that Rajah had written for school in France when he was eleven. The assignment had been to make up a fairy tale that would be read to younger children in the same school. The younger children first read the stories, and then critiqued them for the older children. The little ones had been tough to please.

Jacob loved the story. He called a friend in Santa Barbara who worked for a publishing company. Rajah and Jacob traveled north together to present the fairy tale. The publisher liked it, so Jacob translated it from French to English, and the publisher hired an illustrator to paint watercolor characterizations. The children's book was later published, to Rajah's amazement. Here is Rajah's fairy tale:

THREE FROGS ARE GRANTED ONE WISH

Once upon a time, behind a king's castle, there was small pond. The pond was home for three young frogs; Pierre, Gustav, and Jules. The three frogs were friends, but each frog was different from the other two. Pierre was the kind hearted one.

Gustav was the most courageous of the three. Jules was difficult to please and tended to be very grumpy. These three friends were past the tadpole stage, but they were not yet adult frogs.

One morning the three frogs were playing leap frog near the pond. Pierre jumped over Gustav and then over Jules. Gustav was next to jump over Jules and then over Pierre. It was Jules turn to jump over Pierre and Gustav, but Jules didn't jump. He complained, "This game is getting boring."

Gustav boasted, "Come on, Jules. Leap frog makes you grow up strong."

Pierre had a quick solution, "We could go swimming instead."

They had a show of hands (or rather a show of frog feet) and the only frog to vote No was Jules.

"Two against one," claimed Gustav. They all leaped into the pond, and swam under water to the other side. They floated near the edge near a grassy shore. A grasshopper in the grass noticed six eyes in a row poking up out of the water.

"Dear me," said the grasshopper. "It must be a sea monster." The grasshopper took one giant hop and disappeared out of sight.

Gustav noticed a jewel covered box in the shade of the grass.

"Look at that!" yelled Gustav. "Let's get a closer look."

They all splashed each other to get there first. The jewel-studded box was small, but to the three little frogs it looked like a huge treasure chest.

"Whoopie! We are rich," cried Jules with bulging eyes on the sparkling gemstones.

"Look, a gold rope is attached to the treasure box," noticed Pierre.

"I think it's a trap. It might be dangerous," warned Jules.

"No," claimed Gustav. "It belongs to one of the giants. The gaint wears it around his neck."

Sure enough, the gold rope was actually a necklace. The frogs did not know that they had found a reliquary box. A reliquary box is worn for carrying something inside for good luck. Maybe holy water or incense was inside. Maybe the box held a picture of a saint or maybe there was a prayer inside. The giants would wear reliquary boxes to protect themselves from evil spirits.

The three frogs didn't know anything about reliquaries. They thought it was a chest full of gold.

"Let's open it," said Gustav.

"But it's not ours," pointed out Pierre.

"I still think it's dangerous," Jules reminded them.

Gustav gave Jules a stern look and then grabbed the tiny ring on one door with his tiny toes and opened the two doors that opened sideways. There was another larger door behind the first two. This door had a ring at the top. Gustav pulled the larger door down. On the insides of the three doors there were paintings of little elves with wings.

Gustav boosted himself up to look inside and Pierre did the same. Jules waited to make sure it was safe, and then he boosted himself up to see inside. There was a message on the bottom of the box.

"There's no gold. It's empty," scowled Jules.

"Even the empty box is a valuable treasure," pointed out Gustav.

Pierre read the message out loud:

> Find this message.
> Good luck to you.
> Choose one wish,
> It will come true.

"Wow!" they all three exclaimed together.

Gustav spoke first, "I wish to be one of the giant soldiers in the king's giant army."

Jules spoke next, "I wish to be a giant prince in the castle, because one day he will become the giant king."

Pierre thought for a brief moment. "I wish to be a giant shoemaker, because all of the giants will need good shoes."

Jules rolled his eyes, "That's stupid." Just then, in a twinkle of light, Gustav disappeared. He turned into a giant soldier in a suit of armor riding on a giant horse.

Jules looked at Pierre. They were still both frogs, and they didn't see Gustav anywhere.

"It only works for the first frog," decided Jules. There was another sparkle of light and Jules disappeared. He became a giant prince in the king's castle. He wore silk robes with gold trim and colorful feathers in his fancy hat. He sat down at an elegant table to eat sweet cakes and fresh baked pies.

Pierre looked all around. He was all alone and still a frog. "Oh well, I like being a frog anyway. Just then another flash of sparkling light turned Pierre into a giant shoemaker in a giant shoe shop. The shop was very busy, and giants waited in line to have their shoes repaired.

Gustav loved his sword and shield and suit of armor. He took excellent care of his giant horse. He went to war without delay. He loved to aim his lance at the enemy and knock them off their horses. In the first battle he killed four enemy giants. After the war, the king called Gustav a hero. The king commanded a ceremony to present a new shiny sword and shield to Gustav.

The sword was so heavy that in the next battle, Gustav lost one arm, cut off at the shoulder. He spent a long time in bed taking medicine and feeling sick and useless. When he finally got well, the army wouldn't let Gustav go back to war because he only had one arm. He went back home sad, but at home the shiny sword and new shield made him feel proud, so he returned to the army to show off his shield and sword. When the army saw the shield and sword they said, "Oh, Gustav is a hero. He will lead us to new victories."

Gustav was excited to go back to war and prove his courage. In two days the trumpets sounded and he was back on his horse. He carried his shield with one hand and carried his sword on his belt. He went bravely to battle, but this time he was killed.

At his funeral, the king declared that Gustav was a great giant of courage and ordered a statue to be made of Gustav riding his horse.

Meanwhile, inside the castle, Jules enjoyed being a giant prince. Everyone took care of him and he could order them around.

"I don't like this soufflé," he complained. "Make me another one and make it softer and tastier."

He ate and ate and outgrew his fancy clothes. "This satin robe is too small for me," he complained. "Make me another one, bigger, shinier, and more beautiful than this one."

One day the king died and Jules became the king. This was the happiest day of his life. Now he ordered everyone around. If anybody did anything that displeased him, it was, "Off with his head," or "Lock her down in the dungeon."

Jules grew fatter and fatter. Walking made him lose his breath, so he let people carry him around. His head began to pound with pain, and his back ached. One evening, while changing into his nightgown, his knees gave out. He fell to the floor and broke his arm. He became sickly and bedridden. There were hundreds of nurses and hundreds of doctors and hundreds of medicines. Everyone tried to help the suffering king. They wanted him to get well and be happy again.

Jules was never happy. He stayed in bed and grew more miserable, and even more miserable still. He growled and screamed at everyone and demanded everything imaginable. He ordered executions left and right.

He lived a very long, painful, miserable, and nightmarish life.

During all this, Pierre, the giant shoemaker, worked hard repairing and making new shoes. He hired assistants to help him in the shop, and more assistants to deliver shoes across town. He hired enough assistants to have free time for designing elegant shoes, comfortable shoes, and shoes that lasted a very long time. His shoes did not fall apart easily. Business was booming.

A beautiful young woman giant came into his shop and bought two pair of elegant shoes. She returned a week later and bought two more pair of elegant shoes. She was not as interested in the elegant shoes as she was interested in Pierre.

Pierre grew fond of the beautiful young woman who bought two pair of elegant shoes every week. One week, he gave her two pair of elegant shoes, free of charge. The following week, he gave her a ring and asked her to marry him. She said, "Yes," without hesitation. Her name was Jacqueline.

Pierre and Jacqueline went on a honeymoon aboard a ship that took them to far off, beautiful places. They met giants who spoke Arabic, and giants who spoke Spanish, and giants who spoke Chinese, and giants who spoke English, and giants who spoke French, and other giants who spoke who-knows-what language. They met black giants, white giants, red giants, yellow giants, and every shade of color in between.

Pierre collected shoes from all over the world. He became an international trader of shoes. He and Jacqueline had three children. Life was filled with hard work, and sometimes even bad new, but Pierre had a long life. He enjoyed his grandchildren and great-grandchildren. He loved the world and the people on it. He loved his life.

THE END,

by Rajah

Clam up, don't tell. To use military terms; "Don't ask. Don't tell." By the time I was in high school this quotation could have been the code that I lived by. Redding Junior High School happened to me in about 1967 – 69. Two decades later, in the nineties, homosexuals were told, "Don't ask, don't tell." This mode of operation came naturally to me for the exact same reason that the military suggested it. If you clam up and say nothing, the information cannot be used against you. This fear of information being used against me turns out to be exactly what I needed to overcome later in life. If I don't ask questions, and if I don't tell the dirty, filthy, little secrets about myself; then I never really allow anyone outside myself to help me or offer me new information.

As a teenager, however, keeping things to myself was self-ingrained as a survival tactic, although (more often than not) the secrecy was a short cut to expedite the long, drawn out lectures that were bound to arise if I had voiced my own truth. What are you thinking about? "Nothing." We hear this response all the time. An empty mind cannot arouse debate. What would happen if the truth just fell out of me for everyone to see and hear? "Oh, I'm thinking about smoking pot and getting naked with the boy who lives next door." It obviously seemed best to keep a lid on my rampant instincts.

One of the deadliest sins of my old, outdated code of honor was to ask a question about anything that other people seemed to already understand. (I frequently imagined that other people were "in the know". The word *imagined* is the key word here, because I don't really have E.S.P. about other people.) If people were to find out that I had asked a question, when the answer was obvious, they would have found out that I was a complete idiot. I assumed that my question would be perceived of as a dumb question.

Now that I'm no longer a teenager (in fact, I've recently turned a half-century old) I find myself checking out a library book called "World History for the Complete Idiot". Not only do I face that fact that I have spent many years ignoring history, but I also have come to accept that I am apt to be in the dark concerning many wars and disputes and inventions. Incredible mishaps, great moments of achievement, along with great moments of despair, disgrace, and inexcusable horrors have flown over or past my head without my cognizance. You might say that I've had a very long blond moment. I am willing to admit that in the subject of World History, I am, without a doubt, a complete idiot. As I approach the librarian with my stack of books to check out, I feel anxious and wish I were wearing a mask as she scans the title; "World History for the Complete Idiot". I've already prepared a white lie for her if she were to ask me, "Is this book for you, sir?" "Oh no, Miss, I'm checking this out for my children." Several weeks later when I call the library to renew the book, the librarian refers to it in abbreviated form; "The Complete Idiot." "That's the one," I reply with embarrassment, realizing that the response would more appropriately be; "That would be me." I'm so glad she can't see through the holes in the telephone receiver and see my shamed face.

Back to my teenage story about my arrival at Redding Junior High School: My mother remarried, and a new job for my stepfather required us to move to Redding, California. My stepfather convinced my mom that I should join the basketball team during summer school, being that I didn't know anyone yet.

How I ended up on a basketball court week after week is beyond me. I don't remember being confronted, told, or asked for my opinion. I wasn't at all open with opinions anyway. Somehow, I was enrolled for basketball, of all things. I spent an entire summer on a basketball team without knowing what the rules for basketball were! My ingrained code, "Don't ask, don't tell" kicked in full force. There were guys running this way and that, and guys in another color running to and fro. The directions kept changing. I could tell by the color I was wearing whose team I was on, but if I even managed to get a hold of the ball (and it was my whole desire to never touch the ball) I was never really sure which hoop was the hoop that our team was headed for. I tried pretty much to stay out of everyone's way, but sometimes the ball came directly at me. No doubt, the ball may have slammed me in the face or the head repeatedly, but sometimes, out of self-defense or incredible luck, I would catch the ball. Then there would be a commotion and yelling and coaxing of teammates, and of course the opponents quickly caught drift that I was clueless. They would extend their arms expecting that I would easily surrender it. It didn't really much matter who I was trying to throw the ball to, because there was such a whirlwind of running and yelling and changing of directions. Even if I could have thrown the ball with any control of direction, I was always filled with such a dread and humiliation. I knew that I was just a glaring mistake, and a joke, and a clown. Everyone else seemed so dead serious about doing this dribbling and passing and through-the-hoop routine. I bounced around like a pinball in a pinball machine, and at various times that I had the ball, I headed for the wrong basket. I didn't really know how to dribble and run at the same time, so there were many fouls. The whistle would blow, and the ball would be turned over to the opponents. Supposedly, that was humiliating, but I was so beyond humiliation. I was just relieved when someone else had the ball.

My fear was huge. What was it? I was afraid to ask anyone what the rules for basketball were, because then they would discover that I was an idiot and the information would be used against me. Obviously, I didn't have to open my mouth to be discovered. My maneuvers on court proved that I was an idiot, and a klutz, far beyond the damage that any dumb questions would have cost me.

I know that you are just reading this, and you are not my psychiatrist, but sometimes I wonder if this summer of fear was like a cement foundation for some hardcore fear that remains with me today. If I try to do something new, I might fear looking like a fool, so I conclude that I'd be better off to not try something new. Actually, by this time of my half-century life, I've made such a fool of myself so many times, who really cares anymore? It might be good for a laugh now. Don't you think?

BREAK MY WATCH

My blunder-head summer on the basketball court was during my first year in Redding. Friends seemed to choose me those days. I was still terrified of being rejected by anyone that I might pick out, of my own choice, to befriend. Being chosen did not always mean being blessed. My first Redding "friend" was a hyper little outcast kid. He could have easily have been type-cast for a role in The Little Rascals. His name was Ray. Maybe the local kids knew well enough to stay clear of Ray, and as a result he befriended every new kid on the block who came along. I was not literally new to his block, but I landed in some of his classes. He swooped right in on me like a vulture on fresh killed meat.

Ray was not an unbearable guy. He smiled a lot and laughed at anything slapstick. He liked to play innocent, mishap jokes on his victims. Out of boredom, and lacking any real backbone or experience at avoiding bratty people, I played along with the new-buddies routine. Ray was very much a guy-type boy. He ran, jumped and loved football and baseball and horsing around in general. I played the deadpan straight guy in his comedy circus. He would throw the ball at me unexpectedly. It would ricochet off my head, and he'd fall down laughing and then start in with more antics liked a trained chimpanzee.

One early morning, right before class commenced, he zoomed up to my desk to swipe a pencil from me. I grabbed it just before he did, we had a brief tug-of-war, and then he gave me a shove. I toppled over sideways and hit my head on the edge of a desk. The accident gave me a cut above my left eye that crossed my eyebrow. It took a few stitches from the doctor to put Humpty Dumpty back together again. I wore a bandage and a black eye for over a week. Ray must have felt enough guilt and shame about the injury to back off from his horseplay with me.

The next friend who chose me was Sherman. He was tall and thin and looked very German, with a beak of a nose and sharp features. Why he chose me to befriend is unclear to me. Maybe he noticed that I had a talent for math and

English. I really shined as a pupil as long as I was operating from my desk. Out on the playground, or at Physical Education, I really bombed out, big time. I would consistently be chosen nearly last (if not last) when team captains selected team members. I excelled at the high jump and even tied the school record. Maybe that's how I met Sherman, we were both on the track team.

Sherman would call after school and we would go to the empty basketball blacktop and play one-on-one. He taught me how to dribble. We practiced free throw shots. He demonstrated how to move unpredictably and change hands for dribbling to protect the ball from the opponent. I quickly saw the importance of shifting the ball around when he would steal it right from under me as I endeavored to keep up a steady dribble. As I gained a little aggressiveness for stealing the ball back, he would make false moves that sent me running in the wrong direction as he shifted his path and headed in for the basket. After a few weeks I started getting a high percentage of the free throw shots in the basket. Free throws are performed from behind a specific line, during a time out for the other players, so there are no distractions to hinder the shot. It's no wonder that I developed this skill first.

If this part of my story were a movie, the screen would show and aerial view of Sherman and me on the asphalt court, then close ups of feet and dribbling balls, a progression of shooting for the basket from short shots to long shots that bounce on the basket's rim, lay ups and dribbling techniques would fast forward from simple to skillful. All the while, the trees surrounding the court would change from summer to fall, then winter to spring. The movie would be about a ditz-head gay kid who was terrified of participating in sports. With the help of a friend, he would practice and learn crafty techniques. He'd eventually join the school team, become a high-school hero (after overcoming a few humiliations), and then go on to win an Olympic gold medal for the United States. Hollywood would show conservative Americans that gay boys can play sports and excel.

Sorry folks, the movie I described just is the La-La Land version. It would be considered complete make believe in my life. What happened to me in real life is that once again, I prove that I may not be a girl, but I don't think like a guy.

....

One afternoon, Sherman and I were playing one-on-one and a group of about six guys showed up at the court. Right off the bat, they wanted to know if we'd like to join in a game. Out of Sherman's mouth came, "Right on," and I got suckered into it. Two of the guys joined Sherman and me, making two teams of four players. I was far from a miracle worker on the court, but now I knew how the game worked. Believe me – that made a huge difference. When I had the ball I'd dribble it briefly, and quickly pass it to the correct person, namely, somebody on my team. I didn't look or feel as lost as I did the year before. The game gathered momentum and I actually tried to steal the ball. I knew now that it would be a foul to grab or push the opponent, but knocking the ball out of his grasp is fair play, if I hit the ball only. An opponent was dribbling toward the basket for a close shot. When he jumped up to shoot the ball, I jumped up to block the shot. Unintentionally, my hand hit his arm and knocked his watch off of his wrist. He called time out. We all stopped as he picked up his watch. The wrist band had broken.

He yelled at me, "Hey, idiot, you broke my watch. What are you going to do about it, dumb-ass?"

There was a moment of stillness. Everyone anticipated a fight. I took off my own watch, held it out to him and said, "Break my watch, if you want to." The angry teenager (with the broken watch) looked at me in disbelief, shook his head, and said, "This guy is whacked in the head."

I don't remember if the game resumed, or just fizzled out, then and there. Later, at Sherman's house, Sherman informed me of proper manliness etiquette. "What the hell was that? You can break my watch? You were supposed to fight the guy. You made yourself look like a chicken shit."

In all of my school years, this was the closest I ever came to getting in a fight. I had talked my way out of it. Did my

- 111 -

mother teach me this? Did a teacher in grade school teach me this? Probably both, but at the exact moment that I made the decision, the words came out of my mouth by surprise. I was probably wondering, "Who thought this up?" I know plenty of guys who have been told again and again to talk things over instead of going for the violence. We all know there are plenty of times when the peace-talk approach gets tossed in a flash.

For so many guys who really care about looking tough, what I did would be considered making a fool of myself, being a "chicken shit." I can look back and see myself as a teenager who used his head. I avoided a violent conflict. I feel today, in hindsight, that I chose to be myself, to stand for what I believe in. A voice inside my being told me then, and tells me now, that I was not a fool. Not that time, anyway.

Jacob had prepared himself to lose the gamble concerning Rajah's wild teenage ways. His travel agency had been very successful even before meeting Rajah. For the past two years the agency had been researching possible new locations for agencies. There were already offices in London, Paris, and New York. All of these places held their appeal for Jacob, but they were also places he had already lived. He preferred to try something new. The possibility of an office in Sydney, Australia was being offered to him. He heard only good things about Sydney. But recently a new option caught his attention. What about California? Los Angeles and San Francisco had been staked out as early plans, but now a new venture was being talked about for San Diego. Jacob didn't know much about California except that Hollywood made movies and there were surfers and sunshine and a modernized promise that anything goes and does go on in California.

Within days of Rajah's late night confession, Jacob had laid out his plans for Rajah to contemplate. If Rajah's only real home in Cairo was with Jacob, then why stay in Cairo? Rajah seemed game for moving elsewhere, but he pointed out that his English was very limited if they chose California.

"They will love you in California. There are people from all over the world there. If you want to, you can take special classes for English, and don't forget; you'll be with me and I don't care what language you speak."

"Maybe I should learn to speak English."

And so it came to pass that Jacob and Rajah moved to San Diego. Rajah took English classes and Jacob opened the new agency on Orange Avenue in Coronado. San Diego was very new and clean and there was plenty of wide open space compared to Cairo. In San Diego, and especially in Coronado, people did not live all piled together. The multilane freeways seemed as wide as an airport landing field. Rajah was very careful about his public appearances with Jacob, but it did not take long to see openly gay couples in various public settings. Gays in public were so flashy and obvious that Rajah felt embarrassed and uncomfortable. He retreated back to his reserved and shy ways. His life felt a little tedious, but he refused to return to the drugs and alcohol. He kept his nose in the English workbooks and went out to eat with Jacob. They went some weekends to the beach. They'd bring a basket with fried chicken and potato salad and bottles of ginger ale. They spread out an Egyptian blanket and sunbathed on the white sand of Coronado beach near the Hotel del Coronado.

Jacob rented the movie *"Some Like It Hot"* so that Rajah could watch Jack Lemon and Tony Curtis romping around in drag with Marilyn Monroe at the Hotel del Coronado. The movie depicted the place as Florida. San Diegans refer to the hotel as the Hotel Del. Jacob's travel agency, Luxor Travel, was located near the ferry landing overlooking the bay and downtown San Diego. Rajah would sit on the seawall and watch the planes come in low over the skyline. The airport was so near downtown that the planes disappeared behind buildings and reappeared flying lower and lower. Coronado was primarily inhabited by retired and well-to-do couples. As a result, Coronado was spotlessly clean. San Diego was more diverse with canyons that wedged zigzag patterns onto its map. The area was originally desert and very dry and lacking trees altogether. Water from the Colorado River changed all that. Hilltops were now dotted with palm trees and streets were littered in summer with the lavender blossoms of Jacaranda trees. The world famous San Diego Zoo was a "must see" for Rajah. Jacob had warned Rajah that the zoo was huge, and Rajah enjoyed the gondola ride, much the same as a ski-lift. He looked down at the palms and ferns and Eucalyptus trees and felt he was flying over a jungle.

Within weeks of opening the Luxor Travel Agency, Jacob had located an apartment in Coronado, which was a relief after months of hotel stays. Rajah quickly lost interest in playing housewife. He'd take his bicycle on the public transit over the bridge to City College for English classes, and decided that working part time would improve his English. Jacob tried to forbid Rajah from working. "We don't need the extra income. I can give you all the money you desire." Rajah was furious that Jacob was treating him like a child. "I'm old enough to make my own decisions. You are not my father, you know." Jacob was not about to admit that he feared that Rajah would meet a new love interest, and Rajah felt no need to mention that he had access to a large trust fund, and money was not the issue.

Rajah found a job at a Mexican food restaurant. "*El Matador*" hired him as a host with the intention of training him as a food server after a few months. When he broke the news to Jacob, a literal battle broke out. "If you take that idiotic job, I will pack my bags and leave tonight!"

"What are you talking about?"

"It's your choice. It's the job or me. If you take that job, I'm leaving."

"Are you crazy? I would never tell you that you are not allowed to work."

"I pay the rent. I feed you. I would do anything for you. You are so ungrateful."

"I'm not here for your money. I'm here to be with you, but I'm not a baby and I'm not your wife. I'm not an Egyptian woman that you can keep in a cage like a bird. I'm a free man, just like you."

Finding out that Rajah had a fortune in the bank only alarmed Jacob more. The threat to leave if Rajah started working was his only weapon. They slammed doors and Jacob started packing. Rajah pocketed Jacob's car keys and walked out of the apartment without explanation. He walked several blocks until he reached the rose garden at the ferry landing. Rajah sat on a bench. He felt insulted and furious. He looked across the bay, shimmering in the night lights of the city. A battle ship slowly drifted by, parting the dark water. The deep whistle of the battle ship blared a warning for smaller boats and the sound reverberated throughout the bay. Rajah started back, hoping that the few minutes of silence had cooled things off. When he entered the bedroom of the apartment, Jacob sat on the bed with the phone to his ear. Tears were rolling down his face.

Rajah felt moved to appease his lover and promised to turn down the job. Two days later, he went back to "*El Matador*" and the manager hired him. When he broke the news to Jacob, the battle resumed. "Don't take the job. You promised."

"I didn't want to hurt you, but I cannot give up my own self respect."

When Rajah returned home from his first night of work, Jacob was sleeping on the couch. Rajah tried to take him by the hand to the bedroom, but Jacob sat up, glared at him and refused to talk. Rajah gave up and slept alone. When he got up the next morning, Jacob had already left for the travel agency. Rajah prepared a cup of coffee and went to sit on the couch. It was there that he saw his belongings in the fireplace. The stuffed Pegasus, the small basket that held smooth rocks, the satin covered box that held the yin-yang balls, and the scrapbook of their outings and memories of Cairo. All of these items had been tossed into the burning fire and ruined. Apparently Jacob had doused the fire with a pan of water, because the remains were recognizable. Only the smooth rocks and the yin-yang balls remained fully intact. Even these were permanently charred. The flammable items were half gone to ashes.

Rajah sat dumbstruck. Was it hurt or anger? Which way did his feelings take him? He felt stabbed in the back and he forgot how to breathe in air, how to exhale. These were just things. Useless stuff, true, but nonetheless they were keepsakes. Jacob had attacked what he knew Rajah held dear. He picked up the phone on the coffee table and calmly called the travel agency.

"Jacob, you threw my belongings in the fire. My personal belongings and our scrapbook, they're all ruined. All of our memories of Cairo together, destroyed. How could you do this?"

"I told you not to go to work." There is a short silence that seemed unbearable long. "I screwed up. I'm sorry. I shouldn't have done it."

Rajah placed the receiver back on the phone without another word. Tears were flooding his face as he stared at the telephone.

A MASK I MADE

My name is outdated. The name went out of fashion long ago.
That suits me fine. You know when you hear somebody saying,
"Look at that gorgeous guy over there. How did he get stuck
with a dog like that?" I would be the dog he got stuck with.
Believe me, I'm no cover-of-a-magazine type. I'm the type who
looks really good in the dark. I get compliments, though. I get
this reoccurring compliment, "What a great ass!" I can handle a
compliment. I say things like, "Yah, I don't have a car and
bicycling everywhere keeps me in shape."   Once I said, "Yah,
my ass got blown off in the war. You should have seen the
catalog that I looked through at the plastic surgeon's office."   If
I'm feeling really sassy I might say, "Thanks. Does that mean I
should wear a paper bag over my face?"

My face is elfish. I have a pointed nose, big eyes, and
perfectly arched eyebrows. Women have told me they wish they
had my eyebrows. None of these facial features change a bit by
working out at the gym. Well, there is one facial improvement.
The circles under the eyes go away if I exercise. Exercise and
sleep and good food and the circles go away. I sound like a
nightmare, don't I? Oh well, I've gotten used to myself. This is
who I am: the guy with the outdated name.

When somebody tells me they don't like one of their physical
attributes, I tell them, "You were not designed to attract yourself;
you're designed to attract someone else." But when that fails to
boost my own ego, I think, "Asses are for sitting and faces are
for feeding." I don't spend too much time looking in the mirror.
I can walk up to a mirror and say, "I love you," give myself a
kiss, and then go do something more interesting than figure out
why I got stuck with an elfish face.

Speaking of my face, I want to tell you about a mask I made.
Here in Southern California, there is a yearly retreat for people
with HIV and AIDS. It is funded primarily by the Methodist
Churches in the area. Many of the participants would fail to take
a yearly vacation if it were not for this week long retreat. Every
September, a group of nearly one hundred people, identified as
HIV positive, meet up in the woods at a campsite with cabins.
There is a camp staff that includes ministers and previous year

campers. Many of the campers are gay, but there are straight women and straight men with HIV who attend.

My first year there, about seven years ago, I fell in love with the Crafts Hall. I painted rocks and glued together nature knickknacks and made an origami jewelry box out of colorful magazine pages. I cranked out the painted rocks like a factory. My last day there I cried at the closing ceremony. I was certain that my work-a-day life in the city would leave me no free time for arts and crafts.

After the ceremony, campers were invited to join two staff members for a healing prayer. There were three pairs of staff members, so we could choose the two we preferred. I was in excellent health. I had the aches and pains of any normal person. My healing prayer was to bring my creative energy down the mountain and set aside time to do artwork in the city.

For three or four months after the retreat, I collected materials for my art projects; canvases, paints, brushes, vases, tile adhesive, tiles, marbles, and inexpensive jewelry. Along with decorating some flower vases I started painting acrylic paintings. When I had eleven or twelve photographs of different paintings, I approached coffee shop owners with my photos. I ended up showing art and selling a few.

There's a fun story about one painting I sold, but I said that I wanted to tell you about a mask I made. A few years ago, I attended the retreat and signed up for a mask making class to be held on Tuesday morning. That year we had a new group of Latin Americans from Tijuana. The entire retreat became bilingual. Every announcement called for a translator to repeat in Spanish. The mask making class had about eight Spanish speakers, so a young man volunteered to translate.

I had noticed this little guy riding the bus that had driven us up in the mountains. He was a cross between cute and handsome. I was hoping to get a chance to meet him.

The instructor had an assistant lying on the floor. He covered the assistants face with plastic wrap, making sure to leave holes for the nose and mouth. I listened as the young Spanish-speaking translator said, "Es para darlo un beso." I knew enough Spanish to say, "He didn't say that!" The Spanish-speaking group laughed. Instead of saying that the holes were for breathing, the little devil had said, "So you can give him a kiss."

When the demonstration was over, we were told to choose a partner and I chose the cute little Spanish-speaking translator. He put the plaster cast on my face, and then I put the plaster mask on his. He molded my mask first and after he arranged the cellophane on my face he gave me a kiss. I made sure to kiss back so that it would last a few seconds. It was exciting and bold for me after being single for years and years.

At lunch time in the cafeteria, there were always announcements made. A young girl who was a Methodist minister made a special announcement. She said that bad news had come over the radio that morning. Two commercial airliners had crashed into the World Trade Center in New York, and another plane had crashed into the pentagon. The date was September 11, 2001.

We had no television up at the retreat. Some people listened to their transistor radios after lunch. Shortly after lunch we had what was called family group. This was a small group, eight to twelve of us, and we all met with a staff person. Family groups met daily for about an hour to prepare small projects, to check in with each other. How was everyone feeling? Were there any special needs or problems that needed to be attended to? These groups made sure that no individual remained lost in the crowd of one hundred campers. We learned to check on each other, campers from previous years could help inform newcomers about upcoming activities, and make sure that anybody who needed to see a nurse actually did receive assistance.

On Tuesday, September 11, 2001 each family member had an opportunity to reveal his or her reaction to the news. A woman in my family group had listened to her radio. She started crying and feeling overwhelmed. She said that somebody in her cabin had helped to calm her down and had told her that every person in the World Trade Center had their guides with them. I wasn't familiar with the term "guides" in this context, but I supposed it to be like angels looking over individuals. One young man in our family was angry. He said he was tired of our country getting walked on, and it was time to fight back. There was, of course, the unanswered question; were we being attacked by another country with our own commercial planes, and if not, who was behind this planned disaster?

I certainly lacked any background on this historical disaster. I was not familiar with the name Osama Bin Laden or the Al-Qaeda movement. I knew of Saddam Hussein from the project Desert Storm in the nineties, but not many details leading up to it. What popped into my mind was from a book I read, *The Education of Little Tree*, by Forrest Carter.

I shared this with the family group: In the book, *The Education of Little Tree*, a little boy moves in with his Cherokee grandparents who live in the mountains. The little boy's name is Little Tree. His grandfather invites Little Tree to accompany him on a turkey hunt up the mountain trail if the boy is willing to get up before daybreak and start hiking in the cold, dark morning.

Little Tree manages to get up in time, and they hike up the trail overlooking a river below. As dawn is breaking, they sit still and see a hawk come over the horizon. They witness the hawk swooping down to attack a flock of quail. The hawk flies off with one quail held in its beak. Grandfather tells Little Tree there is no need to feel sorry for the quail. Hawk is doing all the quail a favor. By capturing the slow quail, the hawk teaches all the other quail to be swift, be alert and ready to fly. Grandfather calls this The Way.

This is The Way, which means take only what you need. Do not be like the honey bee that builds its large nest full of honey. By making the nest so big and so full of honey, Bear steals the honey, Raccoon steals the honey, and Cherokee steals the honey. A honey bee is like a man who takes land from other people so he can have a big land. He puts a flag in the land and calls it his land, and by taking more than he needs, he causes other people to fight him to steal the land from him. He takes more than he needs and he invites war on himself. When Little Tree is asked to select a turkey from the turkey trap (a hole in the ground covered with branches and leaves) Little Tree takes his time and selects the small turkey. He knows that Grandfather is proud of him for remembering The Way.

That day in September, I did not see the television coverage of the planes exploding in the tall towers and the later scenes of the massive towers falling to the ground in a chaos of horror. I thought of the honey bees' honey comb, filled with an over abundance of honey, inviting the bear and raccoon and Cherokee to steal it. The World Trade Center is, to the rest of the world, a symbol of money and wealth, and symbolic of a country that takes more than it needs. All that wealth invites the war, because we fail to practice The Way.

I have a buddy who attended the same retreat and he is retired from the Navy. He felt as if his arms and legs were tied. He felt useless and frustrated that he could not be there to help the people of New York who were suffering. His expression of this seemed very noble to me. Where do I stand? I am an American. I am part of this land called freedom. Am I merely an ungrateful idealist?

The next day I painted my mask. That year on the personal information bulletin board I had chosen favorite colors entirely different from the year before when I said, *aqua*. This year I wrote, *gold* and *white* on my questionnaire with the Polaroid shot of me taken Monday on registration day. I decided to paint my mask gold and white. I drew a black like down my forehead, straight down the center of the nose to the middle of the top lip, and then I drew zigzags along the left side to form half of a radiant sun. That half of the sun I painted gold. I continued the zigzags on the right side of the face and colored in that side of the sun white. I completed the rest of the background for the sun, white beside gold, and gold beside white. I painted a black line outlining the lips and the eyebrows and the eyelashes on the right side of a closed eye. On the left eye I glued a gold ring that looked like a spectacle. One eye open, one eye shut. I think of one of the eyes as looking out on the world and the other eye looking inward.

I still own this mask of my own face. It was plaster caste to fit my face on Sept. 11, 2001. I hope to keep the mask always.

WHAT ARE THEY PUTTING IN THE SOUP?

Detox was on Mission or Howard in San Francisco. The receptionist ushered me upstairs away from the screamers and the D.T. cases. Delirium tremors are horrifying and might require a physician's assistance with the possibility of sedatives. I may have had bad breath, but I wasn't falling all over or hallucinating. Upstairs was so incredibly quiet. Except for the staff, everyone was asleep. I had my little bed in a room full of little beds. When I woke up there was soup and bread and lemonade, or was it instant orange juice? Somebody said if you get the shakes put honey in your juice or hot tea.

I slept and slept. We all slept and slept. What were they putting in the soup? My guess was *Thorazine*. Everything was dull and brown and used and dirty, especially my brain. There were some beat up paperbacks on battered shelves by some sagging comfy chairs. One thin paperback was called "*Living Sober.*" The cover had a splash of yellow on top and a splash of brown on the bottom half. It looked so dreary I didn't bother opening it. (Years later I bought the book and read a variety of helpful hints, like; eat some ice cream or a candy bar, and the drink will lose it's appeal. It suggested that you look at your watch and go for one whole hour without a drink. At the end of the hour, do it again. There's even an index for locating different types of trauma or "needs" to celebrate.) Needless to say, I judged the book by its cover.

The recovery home was something else altogether. First of all, I must admit that I bailed out of the whole idea soon after my first exit from detox. I had been told to call a recovery home in Redwood City, and that I may have to call everyday for two weeks or I would be taken off the waiting list. I had read in detox a synopsis of the activities at the recovery home. These activities included light chores, group meetings, counseling, cafeteria style meals, so on and so forth. It also mentioned no fraternizing with the other participants. I gathered that they were warning me that I would be living several months without sex. It sounded like an organized plan, but it also sounded like I didn't see myself there.

I didn't call Redwood City one time. I think I lasted two or three weeks. One day I needed a little "inspiration" to get a painting started, so I bought a quart of beer. I was off and running and back in detox months later. During this time, Elizabeth Taylor appeared frequently on the cover of the National Enquirer. Of course, we've seen her face throughout the years on the covers of scandal magazines. During this point in time, she was checking into the Betty Ford Clinic. Seeing her go through similar trauma did not really lend me any inclination to check into a clinic. A more accurate description of my intrigue might have been called an *ulterior motive*. I had grown up being more the observer than the mover-and-shaker type. I found it more to my liking that as a journalist, or a camera man, I would find it interesting to go into a recovery clinic and "observe" what goes on there.

I didn't work for a television station. I certainly was not a journalist for a newspaper or magazine. I didn't even own a video camera to fraudulently pose as a news reporter. What I did have was a serious problem with alcohol. There was my ticket. I would check into the recovery home for my drinking addiction, and use my own eyes and ears for recording the story. I think I may have visualized myself keeping notes for an article that could be published later.

Let me tell you. Beyond sleeping and eating, one of the preliminary steps for ridding me of the wretched drink habit was developed in a Salvation Army chapel. We sang a song about how God has blessed us, and we were encouraged to speak up and share our own personal blessings. I am blessed because - _____. Fill in the blank.

It's simple. I am blessed because I still have two legs, two eyes, food to eat, a bed to sleep in, shoes on my feet, someone to talk to who listens, an understanding mother, and so on and so forth.

We alcoholics and drug addicts tend to focus on what we don't have. What we don't have we want desperately. We forget to look at what we already have and we completely bypass being grateful. Being grateful for simple things led me to the awareness that some of these simple things are truly miraculous. Two legs and two eyes are good examples of miraculous blessings.

Another important ingredient for my leaving the drink behind was having a multitude of people in the same boat. Bad examples are as significant as good examples. By the time over a hundred people have told me how they failed at giving up alcohol, either I hear a few examples that remind me of myself, or I feel completely capable of telling a few of my own failures. I never really liked admitting that I was getting sick and messy. I'd much rather tell you how alcohol enhanced my life. It was frequently startling to hear how simple the plan was from the people with long time success. They would say things like, "If you don't want to get drunk, don't drink. If you want to be an old timer in sobriety, don't die."

At the Adult Recovery Center, I was put to work chopping vegetables for the cook. Breakfast was a different story of course. Boy did I drink lots of coffee! I joined the "in crowd" of cigarette smokers. It looked as if cigarettes were mandatory for the transition. I switched from food preparation to dishwasher the last month there (thinking that the job would be a little more entertaining, while everyone brought up their dirty plates to me). Truth to tell, I would be the last one there, washing dishes 'til my face turned blue. One day after lunch, I finished up the lunch dishes and stepped outside for a smoke. Sitting there, inhaling and puffing out smoke, it came to me that I was like a fire breathing dragon. Then it occurred to me that cigarettes were helping me to focus on deep breathing. Bingo! I saw that smoke was not what I needed; it was lots of oxygen deep into the lungs and plenty of hefty exhales to release the bad air. Without much more thought than that, I stopped smoking that day.

The counselor told me I was a stoic. I didn't know what that meant and I don't remember asking her. Today in the American Heritage College Dictionary I look up the word *stoic*: "1. one who is seemingly indifferent to, or unaffected by joy, grief, pleasure, or pain. 2. *Stoic Philos*. A member of a Greek school of philosophy, founded by Zeno about 308 B.C., believing that human beings should be free from passion and should calmly accept all occurrences as the unavoidable result of divine will or the natural order."

Was she telling me that I seemed cool, calm, and collected? Was she telling me that I was a cold fish? I can tell you one thing I knew about myself. I did try to contain my emotions. In that respect I guess you could say that I was a stoic.

She also noticed that I had my eye on a young black man who gave me reciprocal attention. She said that I could do better, and she felt I was merely settling for what I could get. This baffled me a bit. My response was, "Isn't that what we all do?"

VISUALIZATION

Early months and early years without drugs and alcohol can be, at times, a scramble for anything that brings relief. We like to call these pacifying methods lofty names; prayers, meditations, visualizations, self-help inspiration manuals, and group therapy. Vigorous exercise helps. Sometimes, in actuality, we reach for a candy bar, milk shake, a strong coffee, or call it quits and take a nap. People in recovery have been known to take two week long naps. I did once.

I went through an array of self improvement books. I don't even remember which one suggested that I visualize myself ten years from now. Think of myself as healthy and happy and successful, it said. What did I picture? I visualized myself, at my best, as follows:

"I live in a stone castle on a cliff by the sea. The yards are huge and the driveway is long. I have an inconspicuously expensive car, but forget about cars. I have a helicopter. The castle has a dungeon, and a ballroom with stage, and there is a soundproof recording studio. I compose music for film and for imaginative and experimental entertainment. I conduct orchestral arrangements of my compositions. I have a wonderful boyfriend/lover/husband (whatever we call him). I am healthy and confident and energetic about my creative life."

More than ten years have gone by. The stone castle and the helicopter are yet to be seen. Even an inconspicuously cheap car has failed to materialize. I still ride a bicycle. I am healthy, reasonably confident, and frequently feel contented.

I am energetic at various moments throughout the week. I have painted pictures and now I am writing. There is also a pleasant improvement that I had not visualized, namely; I no longer feel compelled to achieve success that is monumental or grandiose. I feel more satisfied with the simplicity of who I am and the simplicity of my life feels relieving.

Did the visualization succeed or fail? First of all, my life is not over and anything could still happen. Progress is usually slower than most of us imagine. Do I feel that my life made a turn in a direction contrary to my visualization?

Yes. The visualization did fail to predict my life ten years later. I'm not sure that I consider that a failure. Having a dream gives me hope. Hope gives me incentive. Incentive keeps me going, through easy and rough situations. Time passes, and surprises continue to unfurl themselves. Dreams don't have to come true to be worthwhile.

THE WHIRLPOOL OF ALL POSSIBLILITIES

The spirit has its laws and limits. The physical world holds our bodies like marbles in a cup. "Roll away if you can," the cup dares the marbles. Ours minds are filled with knowledge. It would seem that anything is possible. Thomas Edison, Louis Pasteur, Orville and Wilbur Wright all proved that we can roll away if we try. Try and fail, try again and fail, over and over, year after year, until Bingo, the impossible gives way to a dream. Anything is possible. All we have to do is believe it is possible, and it becomes possible. Mind over matter is a formula to break open a rock hard limitation that molds our belief that something is impossible. Mind over matter may be very powerful, but add the spirit to the mind, and we may have a double whammy.

Anything is possible. By age thirteen or fourteen we are convinced that nothing can stop us. For some of us the magic age is nineteen, but at various stages of a lifetime, we all get these brief glimpses at the wide open possibilities. After years of struggle and repetition, years of living in a rut, a renewing moment arrives when our consciousness breaks free and changes again, comes flooding in and we remember, "Oh yeah, I forgot. Anything is possible!"

THE WHIRLPOOL OF POSSIBILITIES

Rajah is kneeling beneath a tangle of trees, planted so close together that the trunks have interlaced and merged into what looks like one very sturdy tree that holds a wide umbrella above Rajah's head. The lawn beneath the umbrella tree is damp and the moisture soaks through the knees of Rajah's jeans.

"There is no shortage of time. There is an unimaginable amount of time. There is no need to hurry. There is no pressure, no anxiety. There is no shortage of love. There is an unimaginable amount of wealth. There is no need to worry.

There is no enemy here. All is perfectly imperfect. All misery leaves me and is replaced by bliss. I am perfectly imperfect. I am blessed and I am loved. I am love. I spread truth and perfect peace. Magic is everywhere. I am magic. There is no shortage of joy. There is an unimaginable amount of joy. I am joy. Through me, the goddess spirit shines."

Rajah opens his eyes. The umbrella tree is alive and well, embracing itself and protecting him simultaneously. The tree is an expression of God's magic and life force. Rajah feels the cool of the shaded breeze and he hears the whir of tires on asphalt and the combustion engines purring as the flow of traffic rounds the curve where he is knelt in prayer.

THE FOUNTAIN AT THE TRAIN STATION

Arrivals, departures: comings and goings, starts and endings. Everything has a beginning, a middle, and an end; the encounter, the familiarization, the claiming stake, then the forming of habits and the cycles of repetition that become redundant and then we say we're stuck in a rut; the same ol' same ol'. New day, same shit. We scramble for affirmations and positive attitudes; *greet the new day, start with a clean slate, seize the day, fulfill our potentials, reach for the stars, dream big dreams.* Eventually the words fall flat, our grandiose ideas fade into battered old cardboard plans buried under piles of intrusive survival needs; mountains of paperwork and bills, closets full of disguises and our endless attempts at achieving comfort along the way to our next promising goal. Gradually the pattern begins to erode, the rent goes up, the house burns down, the car falls apart, our teeth fall out, our love life turns to hell on earth, our bodies start to sag, the bicycle tires go flat. Things fall apart. We hold on like greedy children to toys with missing parts.

Finally after battling uselessly, we give up, we let go, we move on, we turn the page to the next chapter. We jump on the bus, or stay over with a friend. We run away, or just stick out our thumbs on the side of the highway. If our bank account hasn't deflated, we can close our eyes, pick a spot on the map, and fly the "friendly skies" to a new place, a new start, a new life. We change into someone else - like we're the star in a film. We're reborn, we're rejuvenated, reformed, and revamped. We find new courage, new hope, new dreams (some of us inflate the old trampled dreams). Life goes on. We pick ourselves up, wipe ourselves off, pick up the ball and jump back in the game.

Last year around the time of year when summer gives way to the cooling of fall, when I'm seen again in hats and long pants and warm sweatshirts and jackets, I sat at a bus stop on Broadway waiting for a bus. The morning was chilly. Across the street and down the block was the old fashioned train station, old but well kept. I felt drawn to the place and a longing sprang up in me to buy a ticket. I truly craved to sit waiting on the long wooden church-pew inside, to bustle with the crowd to board the train, to settle down at a window seat and watch the world go by, to see my hometown slip away, to venture out again, to discover new places, new people. I guess I wanted to get away from it all.

A few weeks passed and I found myself there, outside the train station. Between the arched doorways and the streets with cars and busses and trolleys, there is a courtyard with tile mosaic benches encircling a huge fountain. The size of the fountain is impressive, the word Olympic comes to mind. It stands like a huge fruit bowl or a massive satellite disc on a squared support stem that tapers up to the base of the dish. The structure resembles a squat margarita glass. Water spills over in a wide ring, making a glassy see-through curtain. I think of mermaid's hair, and of cellophane. Five grungy pigeons had positioned themselves in two separated groups, each bird either balanced on the fountain's edge or wading near the rim. One strutted with jerks of the neck, its head rocking like a metronome to match his stride. Another bird immersed itself entirely into the pool, and popped back up, all ruffled, looking like a sooty pinecone.

I don't see why pigeons are characterized as dirty, disgusting, and germ-ridden. In Frank McCourt's book '*Tis*, an old character named Virgil claims that pigeons are just rats with wings. I can understand people's frustration with the abundance of the bird poop left on park benches, on outdoor café tables, and on tenants' windowsills. But, if you think of it, all birds make bird poop. To me, some pigeons look as if they are dressed in the silks of the Far East. They look conservatively exotic, like plump Hindu women in wrap-around saris. The hues range from dark to light gray, white dove or carbon raven with tinges of iridescent violet and green. Many have guava colored feet that match the absurd color of their little caper-sized eyes.

I'll leave you intact with your insistence that pigeons are filthy. Probably so, most things are (people included). As I sat on the mosaic tiled bench in the melancholy autumn sunlight I felt a simple contentedness. Unlike my usual sanctuaries, my hideouts and secluded getaways, this courtyard was out in the open in the center of downtown, people crossing paths in all directions; some arriving, some departing, others were passing through. And there I was. X marked the spot. I was at the end and at the beginning simultaneously. As a matter of fact, I was in the middle, also. My story, my life, my loves, my triumphs, my failures, my despair, my headaches, my elation, my stormy times, and my moments of quiet calm – all formed a long braid. Like a braid, my memory caught my attention in pieces, some visible, some more obscure. My sanity, my insanity, my realities and my fantasies all blurred at the edges. This event really happened, this one I'm not so sure of, and this accomplishment I was very proud of, whereas this crazy stunt, well, I dare not tell anyone that I had ever thought about it, let alone actually done it.

Thank God that some things are the past, the long gone past. Today, I exist in the ever unfolding now, far, farther and removed from that idiotic past that used to be me, and now I am wiser and older and more content (and probably waiting for my own padded cell).

HIT THE ROAD, JACK

I finally have four days off in a row from work. Rajah had promised me that he could borrow a vehicle from a friend who was like family to him. At this time I'm renting a room in an old Victorian style house that looks haunted in the nighttime. There is a small balcony outside my upstairs room that faces the neighbor's house. I take my bowl of oatmeal with raisins and bananas and my iced espresso out on the balcony. By nine o'clock I have stepped onto the steep shingled roof that faces the street and watch the students heading off to their college classes, some on foot beneath the giant oak and elm trees, while others traverse in their Volkswagens and compact cars. A zebra-striped bus the size of an old school bus moseys down the street and turns right. I can imagine the sixties style setup inside; tie-dye gowns and T-shirts, the beads and the bedrolls, granola and dried fruit, and the rolling paper and pipes.

Here it comes again, the zebra bus circling the block. It double parks two doors down, and the next thing I know Rajah appears back by the flashing emergency lights. I yell out his name, and he looks up at the tree limbs and canopy of late summer leaves. "I'm here on the roof." He waves his hand above his head and catches sight of me and smiles that killer smile of his. "I'll be right down," I call out to him. Running down the rickety flights of stairs, I throw open the old front door. There he is on the porch steps. My heart moves closer to my throat just at the sight of him. We give each other a big hug but skip the kiss for the neighbor's sake. This is his first time to see my room. "Cozy," is what he says. I introduce him to my two cats, Binky and Bubbles. He sits on the bed playing with Binky's ear while I brush my teeth. "All ready to go?" he asks. I point to my duffle bag, bed roll, and the shoulder bag by the door. "Why are you bringing so much stuff?" "Hey, I'm bringing a first aid kit, a parachute, and just in case we get invited to go to Paris, France – I'm already packed and ready to go!"

He bounces up off the bed. *"Hit the road, Jack."* He carries my duffle bag downstairs while I grab the bedroll and the shoulder bag. Out the front door we're both singing, *"and don't ya come back no more, no more, no more, no more."*

He throws the double doors open on the back of the bus. The doors are painted to look like a zebra's rear end. Inside the bus is not as I imagined. Except for two empty milk crates on the floor, the bus looks empty and the rows of seats have not been removed. I realize when I climb in the front door that I'll have to sit behind Rajah, because it really is an old school bus and on the passenger side, next to the driver's seat, is the usual stairwell down to the double-window door that opens with a crank beside the driver's seat. His luggage is one zip-up suit bag that lies across a seat.

We head south on Highway 101 and past Gilroy. There are rolling hills spotted with trees shaped like lollipops. I remember these hills and trees from a painting I encountered somewhere. Rajah has a ghetto box on the floor by his feet, and he asks me if I mind classical music. "My favorite for the road," I say. Whether fences and barns, trees and cows, or bleak stretches of open land, the music accentuates the rhythm and patterns of the scenery that roll past us: boulders and verdant hills swelling and falling to Beethoven's *Pastoral Symphony*. Sparrows flit and dart after a scampering squirrel to Benjamin Britten's *Playful Pizzicato from Simple Symphony*. Big puffs of clouds ease across the sky as though God were smoking a pipe just beyond the horizon to Faure's *Requiem*. A collection of Corelli's baroque pieces soothes us as we poke along a narrow two lane highway with its occasional clusters of higgledy-piggledy mailboxes. This quiet highway transports me back in time to the fifties, long before traffic got so overwhelming. Back then, freeways did not yet require five lanes on each side.

We come rolling into Seaside with the sand dunes and our first glimpse of the silvery sea. The sun rolls low in a surreal sky. Swirls of glow-in-the-dark salmon and mango tinted clouds gather like unwrapped tissue paper along the ocean horizon. Debussy's "*Dances - Profane and Sacred*" entrances us with its lilting waltz-like twinkling, pixie dust from a fairy's wand.

We stay that night in a quaint bed-and-breakfast motel in Pacific Grove with flowers in the windowsills and quilts for bedcovers. In the morning we take a detour through Carmel, past the white sand and turquoise water. Each enticing home is uniquely designed by a different prestigious architect. This seaside community is Disneyland for the well-to-do. We stop at

Mission Carmel and say our prayers with measured calm and the smell of damp earth and clay rises up into our nostrils. The courtyard at the mission is a wide expanse; it unravels angst and barriers in my psyche. The bougainvillea vines spill in lush crimson blossoms over the walls like passionate relief over the rim of a cup.

South of Carmel we snake along rolling green Ireland hills that drop abruptly into jagged rock cliffs. Massive boulders sit offshore waiting for the surf to roll in and explode with a spray like fireworks. Big Sur is nothing less than stunning. The town of Big Sur is petite; a gas station, a liquor and general store, a souvenir shop, and a quiet restaurant with chairs out back made of twined branches. Behind the restaurant the grass slopes down to a stream. The odd branch chairs dot the hillside and stream bank. There are redwood trees in Big Sur; old, old trees that tower above you like Jack-and-the-Beanstalk pillars. We stand at the base of one and look up. It pierces the sky far above us.

We rent a little redwood cabin further down the highway, and spend the night with a gurgling creek and the crackle of our own fireplace. Outside the cabin is a redwood picnic table and we sit outside in the slices of moonlight. Rajah tells me about his grandmother's chateau in the south of France near St-Tropez. I think the name St-Tropez sounds like a carnival. "It may sound like a carnival, but it's beautiful. I think it's the combination of Carmel and the forest here in Big Sur that brought back memories of Grandmamma's castle, surrounded by the "deep, dark" forest. I tell Rajah about Denver and Golden, Colorado and the Rocky Mountains up into Pikes Peak and the Garden of the Gods with its towering slabs of red sandstone. An owl hoots and we listen to the night and the creek for a moment.

"Do you like Halloween?"

"I used to be wild about it. It seems less spectacular now."

We remember Halloween costumes that we had worn. In the sixth grade I was Mary Poppins, with her umbrella and her straw hat with one little flower on it. I had a hard time looking for the right shoes. I remember going up and down the block of my neighborhood, knocking on doors to ask if anyone had a pair of old fashioned boot high heels that buttoned up the side with white spats. I had no luck finding the period shoes, so I settled for contemporary black high heels. On Halloween day we had a parade at school. I remember two teachers watching me try to climb stairs in the heels. I thought they were giggling about my clumsiness, but looking back, they were probably foreseeing a future "lifestyle" that I had yet to discover about myself.

Rajah says he dressed up once as Amelia Earhart, with a bobbed wig and pilot goggles, seaweed draped over his shoulders and face, tall boots and those pear-shaped pantaloon pants that meet the top of the boots. He put blood stained airplane gauges on his neck and butt and a propeller that stuck through his body, also covered with fake blood.

My best costume was probably the one I wore with a buddy in San Jose. We were Hostess Twinkies. I made body-covers out of foam rubber shaped like oblong cakes. We had white faces, white legs and arms for the cream filling, and we were both in the same see-through plastic package. I painted the official logo onto the package. The costume party was a gay and lesbian event. This was a few years after Dan White shot and killed the Mayor of San Francisco and Harvey Milk (a gay activist) right in their offices. In San Francisco, rumors had spread that part of Dan White's defense emphasized that he was stressed out from a diet of too much sugar. Hostess Twinkies were actually mentioned. It was, from then on, dubbed the "Twinkie defense." We San Franciscans were appalled that Dan White was soon set free. Knowing this recent history added a morbid twist to the costume, and my buddy and I were shining examples of poor taste.

....

We sit silent at the picnic table. I get up and take Rajah by the hand, leading him back into our cabin. We had made separate beds, but we both stay in mine. We sleep well that night in the ionized air of Big Sur. Large ravens wake us in the morning with their raspy squawking. We make instant coffee to wash down cashews and raisins, load up the Zebra bus and head back home. On the return trip I have a thought that I fail to verbalize; that our getaway makes a perfect honeymoon.

THE WINK

My face is framed in back and white, a playful smile and a wink, an elfish sort of prankster with a beret made from a white handkerchief tied into odd corners by Amber. She had me put on a beige turtleneck that looks gray in the black and white photo. This eight-by-eleven photo, behind glass, is a slice into my past, a knife blade in the cheese of my life. You might call it a guillotine that beheaded a condemned person, namely me. Forgive me for not divulging my name. I know this breaks a rule in the book of how to write fiction. "Give your main character a name." I condemned myself and beheaded myself. Please don't try this at home without supervision.

I look at this winking photo of myself with a daisy in my mouth. I cannot see the sad young man who had a plan to kill himself, so broken hearted and exhausted and disillusioned in this land of opportunity. I see only an actor playing the part, stealing the mischievous charisma of a teenage street kid gone astray. I had a habit in those days of befriending teenage street rats. Gone wrong, people would say. But to survive, they knew how to charm people, how to entertain others. They somehow knew how to captivate the escape artist in me. They lifted my spirit when it was sagging at its worst. God must have sent these kids-gone-wrong to do something right, something decent; to help save my life.

....

I took my film class. I was surrounded by creative people. I'd ride my bike back to downtown Monterey and stop for coffee to spark some get up and go for climbing the steep hill back home. The cold weather and fog of Monterey brought back my back pain again and I would lie down in the grass of any park to rest. One evening at the base of the huge hill of the army base that I walked, or rather climbed up to get home, I lied down on the grass and looked up at the stars. I had absolutely no energy to climb up that hill again. As I looked up at the dark, light specked sky, I started crying. The sadness was about starting my life over again, and the hill I had to climb seemed like my life ahead of me, insurmountable. I didn't want to climb anymore. I had long since built a hard earned empire in San Francisco made of music recording, composing and performing; the rise and fall of my own empire. I had rebuilt a descent life without drugs and alcohol in San Jose, with simple minded jobs and lots of praying and meetings. Now I felt like the bottom of the heap again, and my incentive to fight and climb was gone; the air was knocked out of me. I felt no will to go on. I only wanted to rest; rest in peace, as it says on so many tombstones. That evening I felt sure that I would have to end my life.

As you already know, my counselor, my doctor, a Catholic father, and then Alcoholics Anonymous pulled me out of my quicksand. It wasn't as if any of these entities showed up at my deserted island and offered to rescue me. It was the opposite. I had to drag myself along with my deserted island to each of these entities and ask to be rescued. I didn't precisely ask "Please rescue me." What I did was confess that I had this small problem – I was planning to kill myself. The confession in itself let people know that I needed a hand to pull me out of the quicksand. There were hands everywhere, ready to help. All it took was my admission that I needed it.

Years later, I think, teenage gays may have it a little easier. Now we have Will and Grace on television. We've seen academy awards for Brokeback Mountain. We have Ellen. But do teenagers really have it any easier? Suicide rates are high for teenagers. There are plenty of people who still see gays as deformities, as malfunctioning humans, an immoral choice.

It has taken a lot of healing to leave behind my shameful misconceptions of myself. I have stumbled upon armies of inspiration, people who show me how to erase the piss-poor dialogues of the sour past and step into a re-creation of now, of today. Today is a brick that builds a house for the tomorrow after tomorrow.

We are handprints of God in the human race. We have the power of humor and compassion and the perspective of outsiders. We are a gift to the human race. Please don't throw us away like garbage. It is my responsibility to be that gift to the human race, and to not throw myself away like trash.

EUPHORIA

I had a job, paid rent, paid taxes, bought toilet paper and went to the Laundromat. My life operated within the realms of "reality." Rajah came from elsewhere; someplace mystical or mythical: La-La Land, Out-of-this-World, "*Somewhere Over the Rainbow*," *The Wild Blue Yonder*, Dream Land. With a name like Rajah he may well have descended from royalty.

It hadn't really crossed my mind that Rajah had family, or ever held a job, or had his clothes cleaned. He seemed to materialize out of the cement wall as he rounded the corner of the bank. Money grew in his wallet, bills that had never touched human fingers. What need would he have for a bank account? Rajah had no telephone number or address. It crosses my mind that I have manufactured the man of my dreams out of thin air. This thought is disturbing. I enjoy the laughter and the conversations. I'm at home with his presence and his touch is pure bliss. How could I have kissed a mist of fantasy with such passion?

He's invited me to his new job. There now, that nails him down to the ground as a real and psychologically reliable being. He's the counter person at an espresso café called Euphoria. You have to hand it to him for picking a place with that name. "I work at Euphoria," he said. "Oh, really? I'm selling rapture," I retorted.

Hopefully the euphoria is in the coffee bean, because the place itself is a real dive. Most of the burgundy paint is worn off of the wood plank floor, and the recycled chairs are deco-wreck-o, worn avocado upholstery and a hodge-podge of tables. Rajah is euphoria manifested in flesh, with his goateed smile and his long black apron. He's arranging cheesecakes on saucers as he adds the U.F.O. sound effects of hovering aircraft. The spaceship descends and Rajah drops the pitch of the sound effect into a wobbly landing.

I can almost see the black-and-white B-rated sci-fi spaceships suspended from visible fishing line. Rajah is having a boyhood Mr. Wizard moment, bouncing like a stringed puppet as he dish towels the counter. Now the blueberry muffin is hovering, then transported by laser beam to a regular at a wall table.

"No lollygagging!" he mentions as he passes my table.

"What does that mean?" I ask.

"It's what I'm so good at." He's back at the espresso machine.

CRASHING IN THE HUDSON

He's waking up. Sparrows and finches are chattering. His lap is warm from the slant of sunlight across his thighs. He reaches for the plastic water bottle on the worn rug floor and swigs with a savage zest, wets his hands to splash his face and smooth back his straight, black hair. There's a blue sheen to his hair. He takes another generous swig that spills down his chest. Prying himself out of the bombshell, the door nearly falls off the body frame.

The field is a collage of gray cement chunks and a passionate spectrum of blossoms. Making his way on the pink dirt path to the sidewalk, he hears the squeal of an old tricycle. It's the little girl he's seen before. Some days she pulls a little green wagon, others she appears on her noisy, rusty tricycle. Today she's wearing a white cotton smock, nearly the color of her incredibly pale complexion. She's barefoot, and people may call her redhead, but her short wavy hair is really a shiny orange. Her face is very determined, and on this gray overcast day she seems to glow with an aura like a nightlight. She halts her squealing tricycle to take in the young man appearing from the lot of wildflowers gone rampant. Rajah flashes his pearly whites, and the little girl's mouth drops slightly open. They pass each other eyeing each other, both with awe.

It would be a common courtesy to say good morning or hello, young lady; but these days you never know when a parent might be lurking behind a telephone pole, just waiting and ready to file a suit for the enticement of a child with intent to molest. Rajah hears in his mind the overused phrase: children are so impressionable. Well yes, he thinks, children are impressionable, but everyone is so impressionable, young and old alike.

He saunters into AM/PM for his bottled water and the restroom key. There's a business woman buying cigarettes and diet coke. She asks the cashier for a brand that is hard to locate in the barrage of cigarettes surrounding the poor old morning-shift lady: Camel light filtered one hundreds menthol. The business woman has on a tight beige skirt and beige high heels and a tiger striped purse and her black hair that looks like a Halloween Cleopatra wig. The ditzy cashier lady finally locates the last remaining pack of this precious brand, and the Cleopatra business woman calls her a life saver. The drab cashier is a great contrast to Cleopatra, with her long gray hair, a quiet face with large jade colored eyes. On the counter lies her beat up paperback, Oliver Twist.

Rajah grabs a large bottled water and bobs over to the counter for the usual trade off. The cashier turns around with a wry smile, handing him his change and the restroom key. The key is attached to a feather duster. Rajah can see by the bookmarker sticking out of Oliver Twist that she's near the end of the book and he wonders what she'll be reading next.

The bathroom has a cement floor and the white walls seem to beckon, please write on me. There's already a history of responses on the expanse of fresh paint. There's a telephone number for a good time, and the next line claims he tried the number five times and someone else wrote Get a clue Bozo. The word clue is crossed out and above in another color the word Life. Above the toilet is a dispenser for seat covers, and the brand name, Rest Assured has been altered by scratching out the U. Rest Ass red. Rajah never remembers all this dialogue once he leaves, but every morning as he rereads it he feel anticipation for upcoming additions.

He returns to the field of flowers and the abandoned gray Hudson. His disheveled morning look is gone. The housewives and delivery truck drivers see a medium sized slender man in blue jeans, cowboy boots, and a charcoal black shirt worn open at the collar. His straight black hair is combed back, a bit longer than a Beatles' haircut. His complexion is milk chocolate, dark piercing eyes set in clear, pearl-white eyeballs. The arch of his eyebrows complements the sharp angular nose. His full lips surrounded by the peach fuzz goatee make for the promise of a spectacular kisser. His posture is regal and his gait is athletic and yet composed. His lean physic is characteristic of swimmers and long distance runners.

He pushes the rear trunk down on the old car and it pops open. There is no key and the lock is removed leaving a hole the size of a golf ball. Inside the trunk he keeps his fold-over suit bag, his only real suitcase. It has a shoulder strap and a metal hanger hook at the top for closet storage. Inside he keeps high-top tennis shoes, baggy black corduroy pants, an off-white shirt with a silvery sheen, shiny silk basketball shorts, and several V-neck sleeveless undershirts. The suitcase has side pouches for toothpaste, razors, deodorant, bars of soap, and an aftershave that smells like rainwater.

He carries nothing with him on his trips downtown. He has a monthly pass for the municipal transit. Hotels are usual stops for him. There is always a chair or a couch and a well hidden bathroom, and the grander hotels have such well kept and modern restrooms. Rajah has never been asked to leave a hotel. He passes for a guest or a visitor meeting somebody. Hotel lobbies seem to lend Rajah his privacy, but elsewhere; the library or grocery store, a museum or restaurant, Rajah usually gets attention. Both women and men are drawn to him. Women like him for not being aggressively vulgar. Most straight men feel comfortable around him. Rajah doesn't act flakey or flashy like some gay men, and a man can feel certain that Rajah won't be stealing any girlfriends. Women and gay men agree; he's hot.

People have been known to ask if they might join him when he eats out alone. That's how he met Cynthia. The "Wild Woman," he calls her. Cynthia is certainly fun loving and she dresses the part. How she manages to look conservative and show off her figure at the same time bewilders Rajah. She wears wide belts on her slender waist and simple but elegant dresses that reach her knees. Color matched high heels and classy jewelry. Cynthia's waist is the only slender part about her. Her eyes are soft light brown and match her blond hair. Platinum would be too brassy for Cynthia, her hair color is natural. Rajah would not have guessed that she's Italian.

She invites Rajah to her condominium overlooking downtown. She makes a martini for herself and a cappuccino for Rajah. They listen to jazz; Bill Evans and Miles Davis and the Paul Winter Consort. She shows Rajah a video documentary about Mata Hari leaving her seafaring husband to go live in Paris and develop her far eastern dance in her skimpy turn of the century burlesque. Rajah thinks Madonna should play this role for Hollywood: Expensive European courtesan is arrested for spying and put to death by firing squad.

Another interesting documentary Cynthia shows him is about Sarah Bernhardt. As a young girl she became so depressed and morbid that she took to sleeping in a casket. As an actress of the

1800's she became well known for dying dramatically onstage, whether poisoned or of a broken heart. Before the days of Hollywood she became a celebrity of considerable fame. Her fans would throng the piers of her ships as they landed, drawing public attention and making newspaper headlines.

Cynthia loans Rajah the novel, "*Jitterbug Perfume*" by Tom Robbins. Rajah loves it and goes on to read "*Skinny Legs and All.*" He loves the historical background on the goddess Astarte, before the days of Jesus and patriarchal religions.

"A female God seems so much preferable," claims Rajah.

"No, duh!" exclaims Cynthia.

I'm having a bad hair day. Rajah will be here in ten minutes. I took a towel to my head to take off the helmet of hair gel. This looks kind of wild and primitive, like I just stuck my tongue in the electrical socket. I'll let it dry a little before I try again. I poke my head in the fridge and take out an apple and some peanut butter. One slice of apple with peanut butter on it will keep me going until we get to the restaurant. I used to practically live on apples and peanut butter. That and Taco Bell bean and cheese burritos. Hey, there are people without food at all, I was lucky.

I try out my hair sculpture again and the doorbell rings. I go bounding across the living room. I leave music on and the door open when someone's coming who I can't wait to see. I'm playing the soundtrack to *Koyaanisqatsi* by Phillip Glass. It may sound a little psycho and mechanical for Rajah, but it really gives me goose bumps how it runs the gamut from Native American reverence to urban neurosis. My favorite part of the movie is right after being fast-forwarded through Grand Central Station and a *Hostess Twinkie* factory. There is a suspended moment of silence as the camera looks straight down on New York from an aerial shot perhaps from a hot air balloon, or, most likely, a helicopter.

Rajah, as seen through the screen door, is wearing a rockabilly dinner jacket and a leather string-tie with a silver phoenix at the neck. That should have been a present from me, I think.

"Koyaanisqatsi!" he greets me through the screen door. His smile is full of mischief and sport.

"So, you've already seen it?"

"Twice."

I let him in and we kiss. I give him a hug and another kiss on the neck. "I just need to get my jacket."

He takes me by the hand out the front door and out to the car. I think he's leading me to the big black Riviera across the street, but behind it is a two-seat golf cart that looks like a bubble with little wheels.

"It's electric."

"I hope the battery is charged," I say half in jest.

"Fully charged, mademoiselle, I mean 'mad monsier'."

I feel like we may as well be in a parade on the way there, but why not? Rajah is handsome and the summer night is perfect. Whiffs of jasmine overtake us and I think my heart is smiling.

We park beside a bicycle shop and there's a red door that leads downstairs to a garden extravaganza courtyard that looks up three flights of rod iron staircases. Potted ferns and spider plants and cascading ivy come spilling from every possible rail and from beneath the steps. There is more jasmine-sweet air, along with honeysuckles and lilacs and tiger lilies. We sit at a little reclusive booth behind a rubber tree and a colorful statue of the Virgin of Guadalupe. The walls are spicy mustard colored adobe with little worn wood shelves that exhibit wood carvings and clay idols.

The waitress is wearing a red bandana and a long green bib apron.

We order *enchiladas suizas* with black beans and Mole chicken with salads and ginger carrot juice. The waitress brings us tiny *molcajetes* of cilantro, *pico de gallo*, guacamole, and red chile sauce.

I turn down the offers for Margaritas and *cervezas*. I explain that I haven't touched alcohol or drugs for years.

"That's awesome. I quit two years ago myself."

We smile at each other and I take both of his hands in mine across the table.

"May God bless us and keep us free from drugs and alcohol."

"Amen."

We take a moment of quiet and I take in the paradise we are both surrounded by.

....

I tell Rajah about my Salvation Army days in San Jose; early recovery and my first job as an ice cream truck driver.

"The company was called *Miracle Ice Cream*, and one day a little boy chased me for a block yelling, Miracle Man, oh, Miracle Man."

Rajah tells me about Jacob in San Diego and the children's book he had published, "*Three Frogs are Granted One Wish.*"

"The arguments were getting endless. One night, I couldn't sleep. Jacob was out like a log. I got up and went to the living room couch to read a book. When Jacob woke, he started yelling, 'Where are you, Rajah? Come to bed, right now!' I put a bookmark in the book and came back to bed. He started telling me that if I didn't like being around him, he'd go get a hotel for himself for the night and I wouldn't have to see him for a while. I tried to explain that I just didn't want to wake him with a light while I read. The yelling went out of control, so I just left and went for a walk for about an hour. When I returned he accused me of having sex with somebody else. I got so fed up with his craziness, I grabbed my suit bag, put my cowboy boots and jeans and some underwear in it, and walked to a phone booth and called a cab and spent the night at a motel. I haven't seen him since and that was five years ago."

"You didn't even let him know you were leaving for good?"

"Actually, I sent him a postcard the next day to thank him for sharing his life with me, but it was time to move on. The postcard had a big wagon wheel that stood out front of the motel."

"What a way to say goodbye! Well, at least you didn't leave him worrying about what happened to you."

"Yah. If he ever heard what did happen to me, he would have had plenty to worry about."

"What do you mean?"

"The next night I checked into a bath house for the first time in my life. Somebody turned me on to crystal, and I spent the next year and a half partying. The whole thing was just a blur of men and bars and drinking and drugs and more sex and bath houses. One day I pulled my suit bag out of some trick's closet and a small photo fell on the floor. It was face down and bent. I picked it up. It was a photo of Grandma Emelda and me. I must have been nine or ten and she had me all dressed up like some fancy little French doll. I held the photo and I just sat there crying. Grandma Emelda had rescued me from my drug crazed mother who ran off with a musician. I looked at grandmamma's big, kind face and at my determined enthusiasm in the photo. I remember I swore to myself that I would never turn out like my parents, running around doped up and drunk and crazy. There I sat, all grown up and strung out on crystal meth."

We looked at each other across the table. It was not a startled or sympathetic look. It was the look of two people who've been in the same mess and both made it out.

"I bought a quart of beer and a Greyhound bus ticket and headed north. I had a few valiums and pain pills and slept for days. I wandered around like a Neanderthal man for months on end, but I never went back to crystal."

"I hope you never do. Neither of us ever has to do that again."

"And just look at us now." We refocused on the garden restaurant.

"If your grandmother could see you now."

Rajah lit up with a gentle smile. We paid the bill and walked out hand in hand to our little space-bubble transporter.

"Where did you get this thing?"

"Top secret."

....

The moon was full and cloud silhouettes drifted past like an old forties movie. A cruise ship let out a bellow that reverberated throughout the city. A far off train wailed and the city sparkled like a jeweled rendition of the starry night above. We drove out to the beach and sat on the wet sand with some strangers who had a blazing bonfire. Unexpected waves came in like the sound of tearing cloth. Out in the pitch black, we could barely see the ghostly rolls of the sizzling white foam as it swooped in on the shore in the fog.

There are no scrapbook photos of this night, only the memories we have stored in our minds.

ACKNOWLEDGMENTS: BIBLIOGRAPY: RECOMMENDED READING

The A to Z of Classical Music, (Great Composers and Their Greatest Works), HNH International, 2000

Algeria, A Country Study – edited by Helen Chapin Metz, Washington, D.C.: Federal Research Division, Library of Congress, 1994

Cairo – by Malise Ruthuen and the editors of Time-Life Books, Amsterdam: Time-Life Books, 1980

Cairo, the Practical Guide – by Claire E. Fancy, Cairo, Egypt: American University in Cairo Press, 1997

Chambord / photos by A. Martin, by Gascar, Pierre, pseudo. McMillan, 1962

The Chateaux of France – by the editors of Realites-Hatchette and Daniel Wheeler, New York: Vendome Press, 1979

The Chateau de la Loire, by Janine Soisson, Geneva: Minerva, 1981

The Children of Egypt, by Matti A. Pitkanen, Minneapolis: Carolrhoda Books, 1991

The Complete Idiot's Guide to 20th-Century History, by Alan Axelrod, New York, N.Y.: Alpha Book, 1999

East of Eden, by John Steinbeck, New York: Viking Press, 1952

The Education of Little Tree, by Forrest Carter, Albuquerque: University of New Mexico Press, 1976

Egypt: the Land and Its People, by Michael Van Haag, London: Macdonald, 1975

Egypt: DK Eyewitness Travel Guides, Dorling Kindersley Limited, London, 2001

Evergreens, by James Underwood Crockett, New York: Time-Life Books, 1971

A Field Guide to Trees And Shrubs, by George A. Petrides, Boston:Houghton Mifflin, 1958

Jitterbug Perfume, by Tom Robbins, Toronto; New York: Bantam Books, 1984

Koyaanisqatsi (Life Out of Balance) Francis Ford Cappola, directed by Godfrey Reggio, music by Philip Glass, MGM Home Entertainment Inc. 2002, and Institute for Regional Education, 1983

Mata Hari, The True Story, by Russell Warren Howe, Dodd, Mead And Company, New York, 1986

Oliver Twist, by Charles Dickens (1812-1870), New York: Barnes and Nobles, 1995

Quest for the Past: (Amazing Answers to the Riddles of History), Pleasantville, N.Y.: Reader's Digest Association, 1984.

The Shrub Identification Book, by George W.D. Symonds, New York: Morrow, 1963

Skinny Legs and All, by Tom Robbins, New York, N.Y.: Bantam Books, 1990

Sports Illustrated, May 7, 2001, The Wrecking Yard, by William Nack And Lester Munson, pages 62-78.

'Tis, by Frank McCourt, New York, NY: Scribner, 1999
Trees, by James Underwood Crockett, Time Life Books, New York, 1972

Vines, by Richard H. Cravens, Time Life Books, Alexandria, Virginia, 1979

The White Bone, by Barbara Gowdy, New York: Metropolis Books, 1999

Walter Black composed music and performed in The Touchtones and The Swinging Chandeliers in San Francisco in the eighties. After migrating south to San Diego, he painted artwork and sold various pieces in coffeehouses. He is currently the author of three novels, all available at Lulu.com
The Unamusement Park,
Captivating the Escape Artist,
and The Jeweler's Apprentice.

www.ingramcontent.com/pod-product-compliance
Lightning Source LLC
Chambersburg PA
CBHW052139170626
46812CB00004B/1503